FOLLOW YOUR DREAMS

Dare to Venture into the Unknown

By

Jane Roberts

131 Finsbury Pavement, London EC2A 1NT

https://www.theempirepublishers.co.uk/

Our books may be purchased in bulk for promotional, educational, or business use.

Please contact The Empire Publishers at +44 20 4579 8116, or by email at support@theempirepublishers.co.uk

First Edition March 2025

To My Nan,

From a young child, you encouraged me to write down my dreams, and no matter how outrageous and wild they may be, you told me that they would come true.

I followed your advice, and every year, I write down my dreams — still to this day. Writing a book was one of them.

So many of my dreams have come true and have led me to have so many amazing experiences, achievements and a long list of successes, as well as finding love and wonderful everlasting friendships.

Thank you with all my heart.

Acknowledgements

I am forever grateful, first and foremost, to my husband for believing in me, encouraging me, and supporting me throughout the writing of this book—and for his patience during the many evenings I spent editing it. Without his belief, it would never have been written. Thank You, Nev.

To my family and friends from all around the world, who have been supportive of me during my years of working overseas and since returning to the UK. You have all enriched my life beyond words.

To everybody at The Empire Publishing London offices, especially Michelle—your guidance and support have kept me positive. In moments of doubt, you have been there, offering strength and unwavering belief in me.

To Dianne—your insightful questions and challenging comments have kept me sharp and always thinking.

With special thanks to everyone who reads my first book and takes the time to write down their dreams – they do come true.

Table of Contents

Chapter 1: A Leap into the Unknown

'Could you please pop into my office for a moment?' George said on the phone.

I am doomed, Kate thought instantly, putting down her mug of tepid tea. Why would the MD call her in his office? In her two years of working for the company, she had never seen George summoning anyone for small talk. He was swamped and organised his time with military precision; any meeting outside his planned schedule meant 'serious business.'

'Yes, of course,' Kate replied reluctantly, trying to keep her heart from fluttering outside her ribcage. 'When would you like to see me?'

'Now would be good,' came the reply, almost too briskly.

'Sure.' She hung up the phone and let out a lengthy, drawn-in breath as though she'd been holding it forever.

Smoothing the creases on her skirt, she glanced outside the glass-ceiling building as if drawing courage from the world outside. But instead, the view intensified her internal conflict, cramming her head with 'whys' and 'ifs' of all sorts.

Why had I opened my mouth and suggested a 'brainstorming' meeting? That, too, with the company's top clients. Why hadn't I just savoured the exquisite food of the meeting and left without speaking my mind again? Honestly, it would have been ideal if I had kept my ambitions and ideas to myself instead of blurting them out in front of the entire management team. It wasn't as if this industry, dominated by men who

That was Kate's only logical explanation for this peculiar invitation to her boss's office.

However, Kate had learned from a very young age to stand up for herself when it came to men. Recalling her work placements while at university, one experience stood out. She had been working in the kitchen of a 4-star hotel, surrounded by 17 chefs, and it was the first time a woman had ever worked in their kitchen. They were like children with a new toy. On one occasion, they asked her to go into the walk-in freezer to retrieve some produce, and once she was inside, they closed the door on her.

Remaining calm, she sat down by the door and curled up to keep warm, waiting for them to get bored and let her out. She didn't scream or shout, knowing that was exactly what they wanted – a weak, whimpering woman they could ridicule and make fun of. Kate wasn't going to give them that satisfaction. In that moment, she had made a silent vow to herself: she would give as good as she got.

It felt like an eternity, but eventually, the fridge door opened, and she walked out, returned to her workstation, and carried on as though nothing had happened.

In another situation during that placement, she remembered throwing a jug of hot gravy over the Head Chef's chest after he had continuously made crude remarks towards her and her colleague from the university, who was working in the restaurant. In the same kitchen, the chefs thought it would be hilarious to give Kate a live lobster to place into boiling water (that was how they cooked the lobster in those days). She did so with compassion and care, not flinching when the lobster 'whistled' as it was lowered into the boiling water. Kate had always thought it was an appalling method, but she had done it several times during her Saturday and holiday jobs.

At the time, she had thought he would ask her to leave and report her to the university, but remarkably, he offered her a summer holiday job. She had declined his offer. Many times, when she had been serving at large banquets, clients had tried to chat her up, put their arm around her waist, or stared at her blouse in an attempt to catch a glimpse of her cleavage. During that period of her life, she had thrown a bowl of carrots over a client, many pints of beer over rude male customers from behind the bar. She had also slapped one of her bosses around the face after he had made advances towards her and trapped her in a corner to kiss her. That particular boss apologised immediately and formally at work several days later. She was only a trainee manager at the time and didn't want to lose her job. To be fair, this was the only person who had apologised and shown true remorse throughout her career. She had whole heartedly accepted his apology.

Kate had always been thankful for the opportunity that he had given her. The fact that he had come running down to the hotel reception and caught her just before she got into a taxi to leave the hotel.

'Kate, you should have been called out to stay on for the final day of interviewing. Would you mind coming back up to the meeting?'

Of course, she had returned immediately. To get through to the last twelve out of the initial two hundred applications was an achievement in itself, she had thought at the time, and it meant another day away from study and an extra night /day staying in a 4-star hotel enjoying lovely food, a fabulous bedroom and what had turned out to be a great company with the other applicants. There had been six trainee management posts up for grabs. After an intensive three days of interviews, role plays, presenting to various managers and team challenges, she had been offered one of the trainee manager positions.

From the first week of her arrival at the hotel to starting her first management post, she was the one to ask question after question, querying department processes or decisions. Not in a negative way, just Kate being curious, inquisitive and hungry to learn everything within each department she was put in. She worked in departments that were not on her training programme on her days off to learn as much as possible. She had been summoned to the manager's office many times, but to be fair, it had been to discuss ideas, and she had been grateful for his open-mindedness of some of the ideas she had proposed to him. The odd 'telling off' was there, and she respected them accordingly. She had learnt so much over the eighteen months there and this had been her platform to go on and be the first female manager within the group. Even when Kate left the hotel industry, they stayed in touch.

Sixteen years on, they remained good friends. He had gone on to do amazing things in the hotel industry, been the director of several world-renowned hotels and won many awards within the industry. He had asked for her opinion and insight for one thing and another, and she, too, had gone to him for honest feedback and to act as a sounding board.

He had relocated to the Asia Pacific Region many years ago for an incredible job, and she had visited him several times during her backpacking and travel adventures in her younger days.

Kate remembered the time when she had relayed this particular experience to Stuart during one of their early dates. She thought at the time that Stuart thought she was exaggerating and almost didn't believe her. Then, a number of years later, when Kate introduced Stuart to him, her ex-boss relayed the exact details to him and commented that it had made him look at his attitude and approach towards young women in a new light with much more respect and consideration.

Kate sighed. There had been so many similar situations, like the time she had given a major presentation to secure a large contract, and the client had made advances towards her. She pushed him away several times, yet he still would not take no for an answer. She complained to her boss, who, to be fair, stood by her when she said she did not wish to secure the account, as she did not want to work with the man. The client sent a large bouquet of flowers as an apology, but her response was to refuse them and also inform the client that she had withdrawn the tender application to provide services to his company.

Lost in her thoughts, as she walked down the corridor, she could feel her hands getting clammy. Pausing briefly at the door to George's office, she swallowed nervously, wiping her palms dry against her skirt.

Just get it over with. Her mind suggested, and she knocked mutely on the door.

'Come in,' came the familiar, deep voice from within.

She twisted the polished chrome handle and practised a subtle smile.

Inside, George was seated behind his enormous, impeccably tidy desk, but he stood up as she entered, moving with the kind of precise, contained energy she had always found slightly intimidating. He was in his early fifties – tall and trim – nothing about his appearance felt ostentatious.

'Have a seat, Kate,' he gestured to the chair in front of his desk.

She took the offered chair and tried not to fidget. The room was warmer than hers, heated to a near-stifling degree, and the windows were sealed shut against the biting January cold of London.

Her mind flashed back to yesterday's event – the faces of the clients around the boardroom table, her nervousness masked by a forced cheerfulness, George sitting quietly at the end of the table, observing. She had arranged an event with a difference, inviting the company's top ten clients to the Head Office to take part in a 'brainstorming' meeting about the company's approach to service and the facilities offered to clients. In the early 1990s, it was innovative and risky.

Now, George's neutral expressions couldn't tell her if she had succeeded or overstepped. He leaned back in his chair, folding his hands in front of him and said: 'You did a good job yesterday, Kate. The clients were impressed.'

She blinked, caught off-guard by the unexpected praise.

'I…Thank you,' she stammered, her flickering hope reignited.

'In fact,' he continued, his tone measured and convincing, 'your initiative got the attention of our international partners. They think someone with your skill set might be ideal for a new project overseas.'

'What... what sort of project?' she asked, her voice sounding oddly distant in her own ears.

'So, we're expanding our operations in Southeast Asia. They're looking for someone to manage sales and marketing – someone who can bring fresh ideas to the table. Given your performance here, they suggested you.'

Kate's mind reeled. Last year, she'd bagged the award for 'thinking outside the box' and for developing several lucrative revenue streams, but this might have been a step too far. And now, she wondered if she really deserved that award and this new, promising opportunity.

'And where are we opening in Southeast Asia?' she managed to ask.

'Vietnam,' George had said it so easily, so dispassionately, as if he was discussing a routine business trip rather than uprooting her entire life.

Kate's thoughts were a blur. Vietnam was a world away. It didn't sound like Australia or New Zealand that she and Stuart, her husband, had once fantasised about.

And it certainly wasn't the slow, steady shift abroad they had imagined years ago when they were just teenagers dreaming of sun-drenched beaches and cities that mirrored London's comforts but with tolerable winters. They had even made an agreement – Stuart would look for a job in logistics, and then Kate would follow. But he'd never found anything. He hadn't looked all that hard if she was being brutally honest with herself.

She realised with a jolt that George was still talking, 'Say in three weeks, you leave for Vietnam…'

'Three Weeks?'

George had suggested it as casually as if he'd been asking about the weather. On the contrary, all she could hear was the roar of panic in her ears.

'Well? Any problem?' George prompted, sensing Kate's tension.

'Oh, sorry, I…' she swallowed, scrambling for words, her mind darting between a dozen competing thoughts. 'Wow. This sounds like an amazing opportunity. I just need to speak to my husband about it. When did you say you'd need me there?'

'Three Weeks from tomorrow,' George repeated audibly as if this were straightforward. He leaned back a little, seemingly pleased with her response. 'Take your time. We can discuss your relocation package and salary details tomorrow. I promise you don't need to worry about finances – it will be more than worthwhile.'

Take your time, Kate. She thought that was the understatement of the year. How could she 'take her time' if he wanted her out there in three weeks. When she and Stuart were talking about moving overseas several years ago, they had an idea that they would be given around six months from the offer to actually move – not three weeks!

Kate nodded mutely, her body moving on autopilot while her brain struggled to process the true scope of the offer.

George stood up abruptly and walked towards her, his hand extended and his face twisted into a hearty smile. Kate returned the gesture, mirroring his warmth. As she reached the door, George called after her. 'By the way, brilliant brainstorming yesterday. Several of your clients have already called this morning to say what a fantastic meeting it was and how much they're looking forward to renewing their contracts. In fact, one of them is even planning to try the same approach with their own clients. Well-done, Kate. Talk tomorrow – we're going to miss you here.'

Stepping out of the office, she felt as if she were walking through a dream. An offer of an overseas position and significant praise from the MD – what was the catch? Her thoughts swirled, leaving her so dazed that she drifted down the corridor. Her mind was so occupied that she barely registered bumping into someone. A familiar voice brought her back to reality.

'You alright?' It was Claire.

'Yes, I mean, no… George's just offered me a job in Vietnam. Starting in three weeks!'

Claire's eyes widened as she processed the news. 'Vietnam? Wow! Congratulations. Where is that exactly?'

Kate let out a weak laugh, shrugging. 'No idea. Somewhere in Asia, I think. Should I call Stuart now or wait until I get home to tell him?'

Claire tilted her head, considering the question. 'If it were me, I'd wait. News like that is better delivered face-to-face. That way, you'll get his honest reaction. Besides, you know your husband; he'll probably take it better in person.'

She nodded, appreciating Claire's level-headedness. Claire always seemed to know the right thing to say. She wasn't just a colleague but also a steady anchor of the team that Kate had built and a good friend. Super-efficient and fiercely professional, she never shied away from tackling problems head-on. Claire was responsible for a team handling all customer complaints and insurance claims for the whole organisation as well as setting up, implementing and managing the ISO 9002 for the company. Kate truly respected and admired Claire. If she could have, she would have cloned her and packed her in her shipment to Vietnam. Frankly, Claire was the unofficial 'mum' who never forgot birthdays or missed a chance to check in on someone having a bad day.

Kate relied on Claire for everything, from troubleshooting the client's complaints after Kate had originally spoken to the client or corporate contact, to vetting her wild, often eccentric ideas. If Claire approved, it was good enough to move forward.

'Thanks, Claire,' Kate muttered, her voice quieter now. 'You're right. I should wait.'

Claire gave her a reassuring smile before heading off, leaving Kate to sink back into her thoughts.

Back at her desk, she collapsed in her chair, momentarily staring blankly at her computer screen before typing 'Vietnam' into the Foreign & Commonwealth Office website (FCO), where she found a stark, no-frills description:

A knot tightened in her stomach. How would Stuart react to all of this? Would he see this as a betrayal of their agreement? Or would he finally be inspired to make a change?

Chapter 2: Breaking the News

As a company, they had never had any dealings with Vietnam. It was uncharted territory, a blank space on the map of their operations. Still, Kate's instincts told her that she needed to get ahead of this potential move, even if it felt like leaping into the dark. She decided to start by reaching out to her most reliable clients—the very ones who had participated in the brainstorming session the day before. It was a two-fold mission: to express her gratitude for their input and to subtly gauge if any of them had offices or connections in Vietnam.

One by one, she called them, leaning back in her office chair as she noted their responses. Her voice was warm and enthusiastic, and she carefully guided the conversation towards the topic of Southeast Asia. A few were friendly but vague, expressing interest without offering much useful information. Others had no ties to Vietnam at all. But even the smallest hints or nods towards connections were enough to ignite Kate's curiosity, spurring her to dig deeper.

By mid-afternoon, she felt a spark of determination. It wasn't enough to wait and see if something would come up; she needed to take the lead. With a surge of energy, she began drafting a document titled 'Relocating to Vietnam.' Once the document was ready, she transformed it into a polished marketing email and sent it off to their international clients. Her stomach tightened as she hit 'send,' hoping that someone—anyone—might respond with a useful lead or, at the very least, a sign that her initiative wasn't in vain.

The rest of the afternoon rushed by in a blaze of activity. She barely noticed the time slipping away as she ticked off tasks and caught up on emails, only coming back to reality when she glanced at the clock. Realising the day was nearly over, she grabbed her coat and headed out, stopping at the supermarket to pick up ingredients for dinner. It was a quick and focused shop, her mind still whirling as she tossed potatoes, some other vegetables, lamb meat and a bottle of good red wine into her basket.

The long drive home went by in a daze, the monotony of the motorway broken only by her anxious thoughts.

During the drive, Kate rang her best friend, Chloe. There was a long silence at the end of the phone when Kate announced her news. It wasn't the response Kate was expecting, and it unnerved her.

'Oh my god, Kate, you don't do anything by halves, do you? How does Stuart feel about this?' Chloe said, shocked.

'I don't know. I haven't spoken to him about it yet. I am on my way home now to cook a roast and have a chat with him to see what he feels,' Kate said, her voice shaking.

'Well, Kate, you will always be my 'bestie,' but I can't say I will be visiting you there. You know me and travel. Whilst I love our holidays in Europe and the Med, I am a home bird at heart, sorry,' Chloe said, now sounding choked with sadness.

'Chloe, you will always be my 'bestie', and I will be in regular contact and visit you whenever I come home, I promise,' Kate said, trying not to burst into tears.

'It is something I have always wanted to do, Chloe, and if I don't do it, then there will always be the question *what if?*' Kate said, trying to put on a brave voice.

'I know, and I do understand, Kate, it's just so sudden. You'll be here for a few months yet, though, won't you?' Chloe said.

'Well, no, they want me out there in three weeks. Look, we are seeing each other tomorrow night, so we can chat more. Chloe, you will never be forgotten, and our friendship will always be our constant for life, honestly,' Kate said with a jolt of realisation in her voice.

She replayed the conversation with George repeatedly, wondering if she had sounded confident enough, if she'd asked the right questions, and if this was truly an opportunity or a risky venture into the unknown. Truth be told, Kate thrived on the challenge.

For the first time in months—if she was honest, it was the first time in years—Kate arrived home early. The house was quiet and dark when she walked in. She quickly turned on the light. She felt an awkwardness as she realised that Stuart had always been home first, and the lights were on by the time she generally got home. She knew she had a small window of time before Stuart returned.

Determined to set the right tone, she busied herself in the kitchen, chopping vegetables, roasting the lamb and simmering a fragrant sauce, trying to mask her nerves with the familiar motions of cooking. She laid the table with a careful touch, lighting candles and setting out their best glasses. She poured herself a small glass of wine, sipping it slowly to steady her racing thoughts. This wasn't going to be easy, but if she created the right atmosphere—warm, welcoming, a little romantic—maybe the news wouldn't hit quite as hard.

The front door creaked open just as she was finishing up. Stuart walked in, his eyes narrowing immediately at the sight of the neatly set table, the flickering candlelight and the smell of a home-cooked meal.

'What's all this?' he asked, his tone sceptical, his gaze moving from the dinner set to Kate's overly bright smile.

'Oh, I just thought it would be nice,' she replied, her voice a touch too casual, gesturing to the kitchen where the food was waiting to be served. 'We haven't had a proper dinner together in ages.'

He raised an eyebrow, clearly not buying her sudden display of domestic bliss. 'Right,' he said slowly, shrugging off his coat and hanging it by the door. 'Why are you home so early?' he asked, his voice edged with suspicion. 'It's only 6 pm. Have you been sacked? Made redundant? Did George not like your 'brainstorming' yesterday?'

'Hi,' she greeted him with a kiss, offering a glass of wine as she stood, her voice cheerful, though her stomach churned.

Stuart, however, frowned at her with an unreadable expression and took a cautious step back. His eyes swept over the table, the candles, the carefully arranged plates of food. Something was off, and it was clear he wasn't buying her well-crafted attempt at this forged normalcy.

Kate's smile faltered, and she swallowed hard. 'Let's chat over dinner,' she suggested.

But Stuart wasn't ready to let it go. 'No, come on, spill the beans. What's happened?'

Sighing, she knew it was time. She guided him to the table, sipped some wine, took a deep breath and, in a rushed blur, relayed the events of the day: the call to her clients, the research she had done, the decision that she wished for, for both of them. She observed him, trying to gauge his reaction, his expression indecipherable as he took it all in.

'Stuart, you'd get a job out there easily,' she said, her voice calm, as if she were calculating the logistics. 'You could manage all the shipping in and out of Vietnam and the airfreight. I could talk to George tomorrow. It'd be perfect—both of us using our individual expertise while working together and sharing the adventure. What do you reckon?'

Stuart stared at her, his eyes wide and unblinking.

More ideas tumbled out of Kate before she could stop them. 'What do we have to lose? Worst-case scenario: we come back after three months if we don't like it. We'll both get other jobs, no problem. This could be a great opportunity for us, don't you think?'

She paused, hoping desperately that he would look at her, his face breaking into a smile, and then pick her up and spin her around, laughing in sheer delight. 'Yes, let's do it,' he would say, as if it were the most exciting decision in the world.

But the seconds ticked by, and Stuart remained still, his face showing no signs of approval or disapproval, his eyes locked on her with a certain emptiness. Finally, he spoke, his voice lacking any spark. 'Okay, let's do it.'

There was no excitement in his tone. No hint of physical reaction. It was as though he'd agreed out of obligation, not enthusiasm. Kate's heart sank a little as she sat there, staring at him, waiting for a reaction—any reaction. But there was nothing.

Nonetheless, Kate didn't interpret Stuart's restrained reaction as anything negative. She knew him too well. Stuart was never the type to jump up and down in exuberance, to throw his arms around her and squeal with excitement, unlike Kate. She would have flung herself into his arms, laughing, her heart racing with the thrill of it all. But Stuart—he was calmer, quieter, always measured. His way of processing things was more contained, more thoughtful. Kate understood this, even though a small part of her always wished for some infectious enthusiasm.

Instead of the tumultuous joy she had imagined, they spent the rest of the evening talking through everything. The conversation ebbed and flowed, transitioning between business and personal reflections. By the time the clock struck 4 am, Kate realised Stuart's eyelids were heavy with exhaustion. With a sigh, she conceded and allowed him to drift off into a well-earned sleep. However, she was too restless to fall asleep herself.

The following day arrived far too quickly. A client meeting at 8 am in central London awaited her, and she had little time to gather her thoughts. As she showered, the steam clinging to the shower cubicle seemed to mirror the fog in her mind. Thoughts spun around in chaotic circles, jumbled and unfocused, as she tried to prepare herself after a quick breakfast. Kate never ate breakfast, but she thought toast would settle her churning stomach. She poured herself two strong cups of coffee, one for now and one for the road, each sip doing its best to provide her with some clarity amidst the profound uncertainty that clouded her mind. She grabbed her coat, keys, and bag before heading out, determined to keep up the facade of composure despite the racing thoughts that refused to settle. The two-hour drive to Central London stretched long before her. Thank god for the coffee, Kate thought.

Despite the frantic energy she carried with her, the night before had been productive. They had come to a decision. After much back-and-forth, it had been agreed—they would take the leap. Kate and Stuart spent hours late into the night, piecing together Stuart's CV, adding details and refining it so it could support the brief she was preparing for George. The idea was clear now. If they could convince George, they would be able to pull the operation together and make it work—together.

Earlier, one of her clients had replied, 'Go for it, and when we set up an operation in Asia, we will call you to arrange all the staff relocations.'

'Really,' Kate had said, almost surprised when she called to thank them.

'Honestly!'

She was all over the place, her thoughts scattered. She knew she had to focus, but the enormity of the decision they had just made kept pulling at her, distracting her from the matter at hand.

After her meeting, Kate stepped back into the office and reached for the phone, dialling George's number. She needed to discuss the next steps—specifically, the suggestion of working alongside Stuart on this operation. Her fingers drummed anxiously on the desk as the phone rang.

George's voice crackled through the line, upbeat and enthusiastic. 'Kate, this sounds perfect. With your expertise in sales and marketing and business management and Stuart's operational know-how, you'll absolutely take Asia by storm!' he said. 'I'll speak to HR right away and get the paperwork sorted for you both.'

Kate rang Stuart immediately to let him know and suggested he speak to his boss regarding giving in his notice and if he could take a copy of all the agents that he dealt with in the Asia Pacific Region.

'Kate, you can't expect me to do that, really?' Stuart had said.

The silence at the end of the phone gave Stuart his answer.

***

That evening, Kate called an old hotel friend from her days in the hospitality industry. She had a favour to ask. 'Hi, Dave, it's Kate,' she began, her voice steady despite the whirlwind in her mind. 'Would it be possible to use your hotel for our leaving party? Function room, disco, buffet and discounted accommodation. And by the way, we've got a big adventure ahead of us... I'll explain.' As she spoke, she could almost see his raised eyebrows through the phone. She quickly ran through the plans for Vietnam, telling him of their impending move and the bold new venture ahead. The news was met with shock, but Dave was supportive and agreed to help with the venue.

Next, they drove over to Stuart's parents' house. The conversation was just as difficult as she had anticipated. The news hit them hard—surprise, confusion, concern—but after the initial shock, their support came through.

It was going to be a long night, Kate thought, as they drove to see her mum. Initially, she was quiet, taking it all in – equally stunned as Stuart's parents but determined to stand by them. Kate made a quick call to her dad and stepmother, who had lived in Spain since the mid-80s, breaking the news as gently as she could. He, too, was taken aback but ultimately supportive, though she could sense his worry behind the encouragement.

The date was set, and soon, the news spread like wildfire. Friends and family were informed, a list of 'To Do' jobs was compiled, and suddenly, everything was in motion. Kate felt an overwhelming mix of emotions—elation, fear, excitement and doubt—all at once. Was this the most reckless thing they could have done? Why had she agreed to it? Did Stuart truly want to be part of this adventure, or was he just going along with her dream? How would they cope with being so far from family and friends? And, more pressing, was it safe to uproot their lives for an unknown future in Vietnam?

The logistics of it all began to hit her. There was so much to organise and so little time. Vaccinations, visas, full medical examinations. Medical insurance. Duplicate passports— Vietnam, after all, was a communist country, and that complicated their preparations. Kate's mind raced as she made calls and sent emails to all her clients, tying up loose ends. They needed to sell the car, rent out their home, and get a dentist appointment for everything that needed to be sorted on their teeth before departure.

Kate had picked up some boxes and packing paper from work so that she could start sorting and packing some of their personal effects, kitchenware, pictures, clothing, etc.

Packing up their lives into boxes felt overwhelming, as if they were shedding pieces of their past. It was much more emotional than she had expected, and between her and Stuart laughing at photos and various items and books, it was taking much longer to do. The office had said they would do it all, but Kate wanted some input and to decide what they were going to leave behind. It was also a good way of cleansing the soul and closing a chapter by removing clothes and items she hadn't used for years. Not that she had a massive wardrobe. On the contrary, it was almost non-existent compared to most of her friends, including the men she knew.

'Take the emotion out of it, just get on with it,' Kate said aloud.

She had asked Stuart to sort the clothes that he wanted to take and items he didn't want so that she could take them to the charity shops.

And then there was the leaving party. Organising it, answering all the calls and emails from family and friends, each with their own list of questions. Liaising with George's PA about flights and hotel arrangements—details that seemed to multiply by the hour. Every time she crossed one thing off the list, another appeared in its place. However, there was no turning back now. The adventure had begun, and she was going to make it happen, no matter what.

Chapter 3: A Step Closer

When Kate had been discussing client relocations in the past, it had always seemed straightforward – just a matter of being organised. But now, she was beginning to understand the emotional whirlwind that came with moving overseas. Until this moment, she hadn't fully appreciated the upheaval her clients endured. Yes, she had spent time working in France during her younger years and had moved houses numerous times within England, but this was different. This was serious. This was life-changing.

Over the next fortnight, Kate focused on visiting her major clients. She introduced them to other members of her team, who would now be handling their accounts, and explained her plans for the future. To her surprise, many of her key clients responded positively to her earlier email, expressing interest in potential services in Vietnam and other countries in the region. 'Keep in touch,' they had said, sparking a flurry of handover notes and a surge of hope as she juggled preparing her successors with researching prospective clients who might relocate to Southeast Asia. Yet amidst the tasks and optimism, Kate frequently battled a tide of fluctuating emotions. The excitement was undeniable, but insecurity and self-doubt crept in at every turn, making the days feel like an emotionally charged tightrope walk.

Her final day at work didn't go as planned. The idea had been to finish by 12:30 pm and head out for lunch with her team. Instead, she spent the entire afternoon negotiating the final terms of a major contract. It was a high-stakes deal involving the relocation of over 1,000 families to a new corporate headquarters in the UK. By the time the paperwork was completed, it was well past office hours, and she dashed out just in time to make it to her leaving party.

The evening was remarkable. The turnout was far larger than Kate had imagined. Her team had returned from their lunch, worked that afternoon and joined her again that evening. The warmth of the event took her by surprise, and she felt overwhelmed by it all. Colleagues who had once been her harshest critics – particularly the Regional Managers who, early on, had dismissed her with comments like, 'You're a woman, and you have no experience in this industry. What right do you have to be doing this job?' – were now singing her praises. Their speeches, peppered with anecdotes of her determination and success, left her somewhat embarrassed but also feeling full of pride.

The day of packing up their home had arrived far sooner than Kate had anticipated. The house was a burst of activity as every item, piece of furniture and cherished belonging was carefully export packed and loaded onto the lorry. This move felt different, heavier somehow. As she watched their life being packed away, her first thought was, *what if it doesn't make it there?*

Stuart was happy to leave most of their furniture and personal effects in England in store, but Kate wanted to take everything with them. Her thought was to make wherever they ended up feeling it was 'their home,' including all of their books, pictures and photo albums. So, if they were feeling homesick or low, they could have a laugh looking at the photos or enjoy a good book to take their minds off things if they were going through a tough time.

It was hardly reassuring, especially considering her role was to promote and market an international relocation and removal company. The irony wasn't lost on her, and she chuckled nervously at the thought. *I must be a nightmare client,* she thought, cringing as she hovered around the crew, triple-checking every detail.

The packing team was one Kate knew well – familiar faces from her earliest days at the company. As they worked, a wave of nostalgia washed over her, transporting her back to the start of her career in the removal industry. She remembered her very first day vividly when she had walked into the office bright-eyed and eager, only to be shown to a desk with a telephone, an A-Z of London, the Yellow Pages, a pen and a notepad. Her boss's instructions had been blunt:

'Have a good day, and pop in at the end to let me know how many appointments you've made.'

Kate had been utterly 'gob-smacked.' Coming from a hotel management background, she had no experience in this industry and certainly wasn't expecting to be thrown straight into cold-calling potential clients. She had stood there, rooted to the spot, debating whether to speak up. Eventually, she did. Approaching her boss, she had asked about a training programme or some kind of induction into the industry.

He had laughed. Not kindly, either.

Refusing to be deterred, Kate had taken her concerns to George, the Managing Director, later that same day. With unshakable determination, she suggested something bold: a six-week immersion in the business. She proposed spending time on the road with the packing teams, shadowing surveyors and gaining hands-on experience in departments like import/export and warehouse. She wanted to learn the industry from the ground up so she could confidently sell the company's services to prospective clients.

George had listened, his face contorted into both surprise and intrigue. After some thought, he had agreed. Empowered by his support, Kate immediately went around to every department, introducing herself and explaining her plan. Surprisingly, most of the teams had been on board with the idea, welcoming her enthusiasm and willingness to get stuck in.

Not everyone had been pleased, though. Her immediate boss was livid, his fury simmering beneath a thin veneer of professionalism. Kate could see the storm brewing, but instead of feeling daunted, she saw it as a challenge – a chance to prove herself worthy of the position and prove him wrong.

Now, as the packing crew worked around her, memories of those early weeks came flooding back. She recalled learning how to carefully wrap delicate china, watching surveyors calculate volumes with precision, and spending hours in import/export offices deciphering labyrinthine import/export paperwork. These experiences had been invaluable, shaping her understanding of the business and making her not only a skilled salesperson. More importantly, a better manager of her team, offering them the best support and training.

Kate remembered she had arrived at the depot at 5:30 am sharp on her first morning, brimming with enthusiasm, only to be met with scepticism from the packing crew. They eyed her warily, dismissing her as a 'Head Office spy' and insisting that packing was *not* a job for a woman. 'This isn't for you, love,' one of them had said, crossing his arms. But Kate, never one to back down from a challenge, stood her ground. After a tense round of negotiation and reassurances, they grudgingly allowed her onto the lorry – but not without laying down their own conditions. 'You can ride in the lorry,' one of them said, 'but you're not coming into clients' homes or touching anything. Just sit in the lorry until we return.'

Undeterred, Kate took the opportunity to observe and absorb the limited actions, attitudes, approaches and time frames that she could see and take in whilst being restricted to the lorry. Sketching out a detailed three-month plan of action in her notebook during those early days. It wasn't until a week later that they relented and let her step into a client's home. Even then, her role was strictly to 'observe.' But by the end of the second week, she had managed to break through their guarded camaraderie. Through persistence and her natural ability to connect with people, Kate became part of the team. She even found herself invited to the pub with them for drinks, a milestone that felt like the ultimate seal of approval.

Absorbed in the flashbacks, she caught the eye of one of the crew members, who grinned knowingly. 'Bit different being on this side of it, eh, Kate?' he teased.

'Very,' she admitted, laughing. 'But at least I know I'm in good hands.'

Despite her nerves, she felt a twinge of pride. And while she might be a demanding client today, she was confident that the team would get them to their destination safely – both her belongings and the next big adventure awaiting her in Vietnam.

Rewind to her work-leaving party. Kate was overwhelmed to see that the same packing crew was there to wish her well. Their transformation from doubters to supporters was deeply moving.

And now, as they turned up once again to pack up her own home, the moment felt full circle. Ordinarily, the contents of her house would have gone straight into a shipping container bound for Vietnam. But Kate, cautious as ever, had opted for a safer route: sending everything back to the warehouse first, just in case there was something else they might need to add before the final shipment.

The crew didn't hold back on their banter, making the chilly January day more bearable with their humour.

'Why are you taking a washing machine?' one of them quipped. 'No electric or plumbing where you're going!'

'Taking the telly and music system, are you? There are no aerials out there!' another chimed in to a chorus of laughter.

'Electricity? In Vietnam? Good luck with that!'

'Furniture? Thought you'd be sleeping in a bamboo hut!'

When they spotted the mountain bikes, one joker couldn't resist: 'What're those for? An escape plan?'

The comments, though tongue-in-cheek, kept everyone's spirits high as the last of the boxes were loaded into the lorry.

The day itself, however, had been fraught with challenges. Heavy snowfall over the previous few days had already made things difficult, and to make matters worse, the boiler in their home decided to pack up on the very morning the packing was scheduled to begin. An emergency call to a plumber saved the day, but not without adding to the stress. Once the packing was done, the following two days became a whirlwind of final preparations. Kate and Stuart deep-cleaned every room, shampooed the carpets, polished the windows, and sorted out essential paperwork like the gas safety certificate. By the end of it, they managed to assemble a thoughtful welcome pack for their tenants, who were set to move in that weekend.

Despite the chaos, Kate felt a sense of accomplishment. Everything was falling into place, and though the road ahead was uncertain, the support of those around her made it all feel just a bit easier.

***

In the weeks leading up to their move, Kate and Stuart had finally caved and brought in Mark and Scott to landscape their garden – a project that had been a long time coming. For months, Kate had battled valiantly with the heavy, unyielding clay soil, armed with spades and stubborn determination. But it was a losing battle. No matter how hard she tried, the garden refused to cooperate. Eventually conceding defeat, she agreed to bring in topsoil, lay a lining, and have Mark and Scott plant low-maintenance shrubs that would flourish without too much effort.

The decision had been made before Kate was offered the job in Vietnam, and now, as the moving chaos unfolded, the garden project was still in full swing.

On the day of the pack-up, Mark was hard at work in the garden. True to his generous nature, he had also agreed to repair the garage roof before the tenants moved in. The garage had been covered by a large tarpaulin to protect it from the snow, but Mark, in a moment of misjudged enthusiasm, decided to lift it without realising it was brimming with melted snow.

Kate could still picture it vividly – the cascade of icy water spilling over the edge and completely drenching him. She even had a photo of the moment: Mark, standing there, soaked to the skin, his expression caught between shock and resignation.

Amidst the preparations, Kate's ex-hotel colleague had come through with flying colours, providing a venue for their leaving party with discounted accommodation and excellent food at short notice.

The weekend was a rollercoaster of emotions, filled with laughter, tears and plenty of wine. Somewhere, there was a comments book brimming with witty, supportive messages from friends and family. Kate wished she could find it now – those words of love and encouragement had been a lifeline during moments of doubt.

One minute, she was laughing at a joke, clutching her sides, and the next, she was sobbing uncontrollably, questioning everything. What was she doing? Why was she chasing this adventure when she already had so much here – a wonderful family, a secure job, incredible friends, a beautiful home? Her life was great. So, what was she searching for? Or was she running away? If so, what or who was she running from?

During the party, her dad, who had flown over from Spain for her leaving party with her stepmother, had made a brief speech that was heartfelt, if a little dramatic. *He'd stood up on the stage* and joked, 'Just promise me you and Stuart won't end up in a body bag in Vietnam!' Kate had felt the need to quickly reassure him – and everyone else – that the war in Vietnam had ended in the 1970s.

The gifts she received mirrored the tone of the night: some practical and some wildly extravagant. Some were heartfelt tokens to help her prepare for the move, while others were outrageously comedic, prompting laughter and tears in equal measure. As the evening drew on, Kate soaked in every silly chat, every shared joke and every word of encouragement. These moments, she knew, would stay etched into her memory as a reminder of the wholesome relationships she had built in her personal life and career.

By Sunday morning, Kate and Stuart were nursing thumping hangovers and surviving on coffee in the hotel foyer as they said their last goodbyes. Well, Stuart said *goodbye*; Kate never did. She always said, 'See you soon.'

Mid-conversation with her best friend, Chloe, a sudden thought struck Kate like lightning. 'Oh God,' she blurted out. 'There won't be any tampons in Vietnam! Or toilet paper! Or toiletries! No Marmite, either! Or tea bags!'

Chloe had burst out laughing. They had been best friends for so many years, and they had grown up together, really. Had some amazing, magical, fun times and got up to mischief. Stood by each other and looked out for each other. Understood and accepted each other's quirky habits and thoughts. They were 'one of a kind,' and Chloe was gutted that Kate was leaving her. There would never be another 'Kate,' she had thought to herself as she watched Kate move across the hotel foyer.

Kate was scanning the room, looking for her mum. Spotting her chatting with family friends, Kate headed over, the urgency of her new mission propelling her forward.

'Mum,' she interrupted. 'Fancy coming shopping later today?'

Her mum looked at her in disbelief. 'Shopping? You don't do shopping.'

'I haven't moved to Vietnam before,' Kate replied with a smile.

The response summed up everything about Kate at that moment – equal parts practicality, humour and the unshakable determination to prepare for the unknown.

Later that day, Kate and her mum commandeered a trolley each at the supermarket, determined to stockpile everything Kate and Stuart might need for the coming year. They piled in packs of tampons, deodorant, toilet rolls, shampoo, tea bags, coffee, dried milk, marmite, washing-up liquid, cream crackers, blades, sun cream, new underwear for them both, toothbrushes and toothpaste, and countless other essentials. By the time they reached the checkout, the trolleys were overflowing, drawing curious glances from other shoppers.

As they unloaded the items, the cashier looked up, wide-eyed and quipped, 'Are you setting up a corner shop?'

'No,' Kate's mum replied with a laugh. 'My daughter's off to Vietnam.'

The cashier raised an eyebrow, as if they'd just announced that she was moving to the moon.

Kate and her mum somehow managed to get all of the shopping into Kate's company car with no room to spare.

The following day, Kate drove the loaded car to the warehouse. Wearing her high viz jacket, she walked into the office, where Gary, the warehouse manager, greeted her with a grin.

'Hi, Gary,' she said, gesturing to the car. 'Any chance I can add this lot to my shipment?'

Gary leaned out of the doorway and chuckled amusingly when he saw the mountain of goods in the flattened back seat and boot, 'What on earth, Kate? Have you cleared out the supermarket? You setting up shop there too?'

'Something like that,' she replied, giggling.

Gary called over a couple of crew to help pack, box up and load the items into the shipping container. As Kate turned to leave, he grinned and said, 'Good luck! Break a leg out there!'

Kate smiled her thanks before heading back to the company car, which she was allowed to keep until the day before she left the UK. Next on the agenda was picking up her dad and stepmother to take them to the airport.

Now, as she dropped them off at the airport, saying 'see you soon' to her dad proved far harder than she'd anticipated. Tears streamed down her cheeks as she hugged him tightly, her chest aching with the weight of the goodbye. She knew he would never visit Vietnam—he wasn't the sort to venture that far—and unless she made sure to visit Spain whenever she was back in Europe, it might be years before they saw each other again.

The drive back to Stuart's parents' house was a blur of tears and quiet sobs, the emotional toll of the past weeks catching up with her.

That night, Kate finally collapsed in a heap. The adrenaline that had kept her going through the chaos of the last two and a half weeks drained away, leaving her utterly spent. For the first time in what felt like forever, she surrendered to the overwhelming exhaustion and slept deeply, the tumult of emotions momentarily silenced by a sound slumber.

Chapter 4: The Gateway to New Adventures

The next morning, Stuart's mum approached Kate with a question that felt redolent of their imminent departure:

'What would you like for your last dinner?'

'It's not our last dinner,' Kate blurted out, struggling to hold back a sob. Her voice wavered, but she managed to compose herself. 'We'll be coming back to see you all, and I'll be writing to you and telephoning frequently,' she added, attempting a subtle smile.

Kate knew deep down that neither of Stuart's parents would ever venture out to visit them. Travelling just wasn't their thing. America, yes, but Asia? Vietnam? Absolutely not. It was too far, too unfamiliar and far too outside their comfort zone.

But Liz—Stuart's sister—was different. Kate was certain she would make the journey. Liz loved to travel, and Kate adored her for it. Over the years, they had shared countless moments of joy, laughter and adventures. They were the perfect pair of companions, not just sisters-in-law but close friends. Kate and Stuart had even holidayed with Liz and her husband on several occasions, memories that Kate now held dear.

Liz was everything Stuart wasn't: vivacious, adventurous and endlessly outgoing. She embraced life with an infectious enthusiasm, always up for a laugh and the next great experience. Only six months younger than Kate, their bond had strengthened naturally over the years as Kate and Stuart's relationship blossomed.

Sitting at the kitchen table, Kate's gaze drifted upward to the wall opposite her. Jenny, Stuart's mother, had carefully arranged an assortment of family photographs along its length. Each picture was beautifully framed and grouped together, chronicling significant family milestones. Among them, Kate's eyes landed on their wedding photos—perfectly centred and prominently displayed.

The sight gave Kate pause. For some reason, it transported her back to that time in her life. She remembered it vividly, though the emotions it stirred were complex.

Kate had never been religious. She was christened a Christian but had never truly believed, nor did she follow the faith. Stuart and his family, on the other hand, were Catholic, though they were not practising. Despite their differing views, Stuart had always been keen to marry.

At the time, Kate couldn't understand the fuss. To her, marriage was just a formality—a piece of paper. If two people truly wanted to spend their lives together, why did they need a certificate to prove it? But she recognized the practicalities. There were legal and financial protections, especially if they ever decided to have children.

Eventually, after much discussion, they'd agreed to marry, though on their terms. There would be no religious ceremony, no church and most definitely no white dress. Kate had been adamant about that. She'd made it clear to Stuart: their wedding would reflect them as a couple, not the weight of tradition.

Kate remembered the way they'd discussed the basics: the date, the type of venue, all of it decided quickly in February. They planned to marry that June—just a few short months away. Neither she nor Stuart saw the point in dragging things out. Unlike so many couples they knew, who had spent a year—sometimes nearly three—obsessively planning every last detail of their 'big day,' Kate couldn't imagine anything worse. It wasn't her style.

She had turned to her trusted network in the hotel industry and found the ideal venue without fuss: a beautiful woodland area tucked within the grounds of a charming countryside hotel for their ceremony. The hotel could host both the ceremony and the reception, and there were more than enough rooms for family and friends to stay overnight—at a generous discount Kate had negotiated with the owner, Cliff (an ex-director of a hotel she had managed). Practical, simple and sorted.

For music, she arranged a string quartet—something tasteful but non-religious—to play as guests arrived, as she walked down the 'aisle' during the ceremony, and while guests enjoyed drinks afterwards. Kate's godmother, a registrar by profession, had kindly offered to conduct the ceremony. It was a lovely, personal touch that meant the world to Kate.

Then there were the photos. Liz, always full of good ideas, suggested her friend—a photographer from the newspaper she worked for. He wasn't like the typical wedding photographer, stiff and formal, but instead had a knack for capturing moments as they naturally unfolded. 'He'll just float around,' Liz had promised. 'You won't even know he's there.' Stuart, predictably, had asked for a few organised group shots, but otherwise, Kate thought it sounded perfect. She hated having her picture taken. The idea of natural, candid shots suited her down to the ground.

With the essentials in place, the invitations were sent out. Kate promptly shoved 'the wedding' to the back of her mind. She had no desire to spend months agonising over details. But inevitably, her mother and friends badgered her into submission regarding her wedding dress.

Her mum insisted they go shopping – not a successful day for Kate. Her mum knew how much she hated shopping, particularly clothes shopping. She just made the most of her time spent with Kate. They had enjoyed spending time together even if it was a somewhat stressful and unsuccessful day. Then her stepmother joined in, too, on another day. Together, they headed out for a day of dress hunting. Within an hour, Kate's resolve crumbled. She and her stepmother ended up abandoning the whole endeavour and spent the rest of the day at a fantastic little restaurant in Camden, eating, drinking and laughing instead. It was far more enjoyable than combing through racks of frilly gowns. It hadn't felt as though she had wasted yet another precious day off 'dress shopping.'

Weeks passed, and Kate still hadn't made much effort. Eventually, in exasperation, she jokingly said to Stuart's mum, Jenny, 'Honestly, I'll just turn up in jeans. Why change a habit of a lifetime?' She'd laughed, but Jenny wasn't having any of it.

'Right,' Jenny declared, 'we're going dress shopping.' And with that, Kate was whisked away to Windsor.

It was a full day of searching. Kate tried on dress after dress, each one more unsuitable than the last. Too much lace. Too much sparkle. Everything felt far too *girlie* and frilly for her taste. By late afternoon, her patience had run dry. 'I'm done,' she sighed to Jenny.

But Jenny wasn't ready to give up. As they left the final shop, Jenny spotted a small fabric and pattern store across the road. 'Come on,' she said brightly. 'If we can't find one, we'll *make* one.'

Out of options, Kate followed her inside. The shop was overflowing with rolls of fabric and shelves stacked with sewing patterns. Kate's heart sank as her eyes skimmed through the pattern books, looking at the selection. Most of the patterns were big, flouncy and completely over-the-top dresses—nothing like the sleek, simple and understated look she had in mind.

She was about to turn on her heel and leave when a woman approached them.

'Looking for something in particular?' the woman asked kindly, her voice cutting through Kate's frustration.

Kate hesitated, glancing at Jenny, who smiled as if to say, *Let's see where this goes.*

And for the first time that day, Kate allowed herself to hope that maybe—just maybe—she might find something after all.

'I'm a dressmaker. I live just over the road. Why don't you come round for a cup of tea and tell me exactly what style of dress you're after? What have you got to lose—an hour of your time?'

The petite woman's words melted the tense moment, and Kate and Jenny exchanged glances, both surprised but intrigued. There was an unspoken agreement between them. 'All right,' Jenny said finally, and they followed the woman out of the shop.

For the life of her, Kate could never quite recall the woman's name. But she remembered *her*—the image of her was crystal clear even now. She had been immaculately put together, as if she'd stepped straight from a bygone era: petite, with hair swept up into a neat bun, every strand perfectly in place. Her makeup was minimal but polished, and her eyes sparkled with quiet delight when they had agreed to go to her home.

They followed her across the cobbled streets, through an arched gate, and into a row of quaint cottages nestled just inside the grounds of Windsor Castle. The place seemed almost magical, tucked away in its own little corner of history. The woman's cottage was small but utterly charming—warm, inviting, and filled with an understated elegance.

Once inside, she offered them tea, which they gratefully accepted, and Kate found herself relaxing in the cosy surroundings. The woman fetched a notepad and pencil, pulling a chair up to the little kitchen table. 'Now,' she said gently, 'tell me what you're imagining.'

Kate began describing her vision, at first hesitantly, as if unsure how to put it into words. But the woman nodded encouragingly, and soon the ideas tumbled out. All the while, her host's hand moved effortlessly across the paper, her pencil gliding in smooth, confident strokes. It was mesmerising to watch.

When the woman turned the pad towards Kate, her heart skipped a beat. There it was—the dress she had imagined, brought to life in perfect detail. A scalloped low collar framed her collarbones elegantly, capped shoulder sleeves that gave a delicate touch, and a slim-fitting bodice flared into a fishtail train. Kate smiled at the thought of swishing the trail behind her, pretending—just for one day—that she was the height of femininity and grace.

'And fingerless gloves,' she had added eagerly. 'Silk ones, up to the elbow. Very elegant.'

The woman nodded, sketching quickly. 'And the colour?'

'Not white,' Kate said firmly. 'Something soft—perhaps a very pale salmon pink, in silk.'

She went on to describe the final piece of the look: no veil, but instead a wide-brimmed straw-effect hat. 'I'd want natural flowers—fresh ones—woven around the brim. And perhaps a strip of that same salmon silk to tie it all together. Simple but elegant.'

She remembered Jenny bursting into laughter alongside her, both of them giddy with excitement. Kate had hardly expected anyone to take her idea seriously, much less sketch it with such precision and artistry.

A price was discussed, and Kate had blinked in disbelief. It was so reasonable—*ridiculously* so—that she had to ask, 'Are you sure? Have I misheard?'

The woman looked up, her pencil still for a moment. Her voice was soft but sincere as she replied, 'It will be my absolute pleasure to do this for you. It's not about the money.'

There was something so genuine about her tone that it left Kate momentarily speechless. But the question on her lips—

and Jenny's too, she was certain—finally bubbled up. 'How come you're living here? In the grounds of Windsor Castle?'

The woman didn't even look up, her hand still moving fluidly across the paper as if the question had barely registered. She answered casually, almost offhand, 'I'm the seamstress for the Queen.'

Kate and Jenny stared at her, mouths slightly agape, then turned to look at each other in astonishment. The *Queen's* seamstress? Here, offering tea and drawing *her* a dress?

Kate could hardly believe her luck. She left the little cottage that day with a sketch of the perfect wedding dress and the quiet certainty that, despite the tight one week to the fitting and two-week to complete deadline, she was in the hands of someone truly extraordinary.

Two weeks later, on the eve of her wedding, Kate found herself finishing work late. It was gone 6 p.m. by the time she arrived at the hotel, feeling drained but relieved that Jenny had kindly collected the dress for her earlier that day. The plan was simple: she'd check in, have a quiet evening with her mum, Chloe, Jenny, Liz, her grandmother and her stepmother, and marry Stuart the next morning.

It was a Friday wedding—unconventional but fitting for them.

As she pulled into the driveway, Stuart came running out to meet her. His expression instantly wiped the smile from her face.

'Hi,' she said cautiously, her voice light but uncertain. The look on Stuart's face—wide-eyed and tense—set alarm bells ringing. 'What's happened?'

'You need to come and see where we're supposed to be getting married tomorrow,' he said breathlessly.

Kate frowned. 'What do you mean? It's in the woods, in the glade. What could possibly be wrong, Stuart?'

He didn't answer. He simply grabbed her hand and muttered, 'Just come and take a look.'

They walked across the grounds in silence. When they reached the glade, Kate froze. The sight before her was unrecognizable. What had once been a picturesque clearing surrounded by trees was now flattened earth, concrete foundations, and half-constructed brickwork. It was a bloody building site.

Kate's shock quickly turned to fury. Shaking her hand free from Stuart's, she spun around and marched back toward the hotel, her heels clattering furiously on the gravel. Bursting into the reception, she demanded to see the owner—Cliff—an ex-director she had once worked for when he'd run another hotel. Now he owned this one, and Kate expected answers. Kate jokingly said during their meeting when she and Stuart met him back in February, 'Don't build any more rooms until we have had our wedding ceremony here in the woods.' She was only joking when she said it – this was a nightmare.

'I want to see Cliff. Now,' she said, her voice low and controlled but seething with anger.

The reception staff, clearly flustered, tried to placate her, but Kate wasn't having it. 'Please get me *Cliff*,' she repeated.

It was Max who finally appeared. His usual air of confidence had vanished. He looked down at his shoes, shuffling nervously before meeting her glare.

'What the hell is going on, Max?' Kate cried, her voice rising. 'Why didn't anyone tell us? We're supposed to be getting married there tomorrow, and it's a bloody *building site*!'

Max looked utterly defeated. He sighed, running a hand through his thinning hair before muttering, 'I was told not to tell you. If I'd said anything, I'd have been sacked. I'm so, so sorry, Kate. Truly.'

For a moment, the anger flared hotter in Kate's chest. She and Max had worked together for several years in another hotel. He had then joined the director, Cliff, when he opened his own hotel. She could not understand why Max had not even given her a hint so she could have come up weeks ago and sorted things.

But true to form, she forced the emotion aside. She was nothing if not practical in a crisis, and fury wouldn't solve this mess. Taking a deep breath, she switched into what Stuart called her 'damage limitation mode.'

'Right,' she said, all business now. 'Here's what's going to happen. First thing tomorrow morning, you, Max, me, Stuart, and his best man are going to drive around the bloody countryside until we find somewhere—*anywhere*—to hold the ceremony.' Her tone was full of controlled emotion and hurt, no argument.

Max nodded, his relief palpable. He knew better than to argue with Kate. Her hurt overwhelmed him, if truth be told.

With the plan set, Kate & Stuart had made a quick round of stops to see Stuart's parents, her mum, dad and step-mum, calmly explaining the situation. They were shocked, of course, but if Kate's unflappable attitude had taught them anything, it was that things would somehow work out.

By the time they returned to the hotel bar, she was tired but resolute. Giving Stuart a quick kiss, she turned to Max, who hovered nearby, looking thoroughly miserable.

'Take me to the local pub,' she said, her tone flat but pointed. 'The least you can do is buy me *many* drinks.'

Max, realizing she meant it, simply nodded. 'I'll arrange a taxi to take us.

And so, on the eve of her wedding, with chaos swirling around her, Kate went to the pub with Max, still fuming, and they drank until the mess of the day blurred into laughter. Tomorrow, somehow, she would fix it. But for tonight, she would let herself laugh, drink and forget—just for a little while.

Kate laughed to herself as she remembered that night— the night before her wedding—when she'd ended up far too drunk. She hadn't eaten properly for days, not since the morning two days prior, and the drinks had hit her hard. It was 4 a.m. by the time she stumbled back into the hotel room she was sharing with her mum, a tradition in those days. Feeling the effects of too much alcohol and far too little food, she sat on the edge of the bed and sipped a few cups of lukewarm coffee, nibbling on the dry biscuits provided by the hotel. Her head spun, her stomach grumbled, and sleep refused to come.

She tossed and turned, her mind racing with what the morning might bring. Her mum had woken up, annoyed with her for being out so late, and remarked on how awful she looked. Kate had told her to go back to sleep and see her at the wedding.

At 6 a.m., with just two hours of restless nothingness behind her, Kate finally gave up on sleep. By 6.30 a.m., she, Stuart, Max and Stuart's best man were already on the road in a mini-bus, desperately searching for somewhere—*anywhere*—to get married later that day.

They drove from place to place, in and out of village halls and country houses, all with no success. It was starting to feel hopeless. By 12.30 p.m., exhaustion and frustration had set in. Kate slumped in the back seat of the mini-bus, staring blankly out of the window. Ironically, the radio began to play *'Going to the Chapel and We're Gonna Get Married.'* She couldn't help but laugh bitterly. At this point, she was resigned to the reality of getting married on a building site surrounded by scaffolding and half-laid brick walls.

Then, Max's voice called out from the front. 'There's one more place—on the way back. No harm in trying.'

They arrived at a small, stately property, peacocks walking gracefully in the grounds. The gift shop attendant kindly but apologetically explained, 'I can't make that kind of decision when they asked if they could hold their wedding ceremony there. The manager's out buying peacock food. She'll be back in about an hour.'

'That'll be too late,' Kate replied quietly as her eyes welled up with tears. Forcing a polite smile. 'Thank you anyway.'

Disappointed, they climbed back into the mini-bus. As they drove slowly back down the long driveway, a car appeared, coming towards them on the opposite side. Kate sat up sharply. 'Pull over, Max—this has to be her!'

As the minibus came to a stop, Kate leapt out before it had even fully parked. She hurried over, her heart pounding and saw a woman in the driver's seat. Kate didn't even pause to breathe.

'Excuse me,' she said, tears spilling down her cheeks as she spoke. 'Are you the manager here? Can we have our wedding ceremony here, please—*today?*'

The woman looked startled, and Kate pressed on. 'We have a registrar. A quartet. A photographer. We can bring the 67 chairs from the hotel, tables, everything. Please,' she pleaded, her glistening eyes full of hope and desperation.

The woman hesitated for a split second, doubt flickering across her face. Then, to Kate's astonishment, she smiled and said, 'Yes.'

'Yes?' Kate echoed in disbelief, as relief washed over her.

'What time's the ceremony?' the manager asked.

'Three o'clock,' Kate replied, wiping her tear-streaked cheeks.

'Oh, my goodness,' the woman said, glancing at her watch. 'In one and a half hours?'

As Kate turned back to climb into the mini-bus, she paused, turning over one last thought. 'Would you mind if we brought some bubbly for our family and friends after the ceremony? And maybe had some informal photos taken here?'

'No problem at all,' the woman replied warmly. 'As long as I can get the local newspaper here. You know, the last wedding held here was in the 1700s—this is quite the occasion! And don't worry about chairs or tables. We've got plenty here.'

Kate could have hugged her. Instead, she climbed back into the mini-bus and turned to Max. 'Make sure there's a 52-seater coach outside the hotel at 2.30 p.m. sharp to bring our family and friends here. And for God's sake, make it look like this was *pre-planned*. I don't want anyone thinking this was a last-minute panic because your boss turned our venue into a bloody building site.'

Max nodded, his face flushed with shame and concern as to how he could pull this request off at such short notice – nearly impossible, he quietly said to himself, knowing he had to achieve it.

Looking back now, Kate was glad she'd never been the 'girly-girly' type who had squarely planned a day of pampering with hairdressers, makeup artists and florists. It saved her a lot of hassle and chaos. Her mum, of course, wasn't thrilled about being left out of the frantic morning escapades, but Kate explained later that there simply hadn't been time to involve anyone.

Her mum had kindly done her hair, twisting and pinning it into something simple and presentable. The dress, though, felt two sizes too big when she put it on—it was unsurprising, given she'd hardly eaten or slept in days. She must have dropped several pounds, though she hadn't noticed until now.

She caught her reflection in the mirror and sighed.

Her eyes were puffy and swollen from tears and exhaustion. Her face was red and spotty from her crying and lack of sleep.

Just this once, she wanted to be a beautiful, stunning-looking lady free of any worries and, heaven forbid, enjoy just a little pampering time.

Get on with it, she had told herself whilst she stared at the mirror.

Maybe, she thought, there was something stronger at play. Perhaps she had never been destined to have a perfectly relaxed, stress-free, fairy-tale wedding day. Maybe she wasn't supposed to get married. Was this a sign?

Kate could remember every single detail of that day with absolute clarity. It was as if the entire sequence of events had been etched permanently into her mind.

Her father-in-law had been the one to drive her and her dad to Kirby Hall for the ceremony. True to his word, Max had delivered: the coach had arrived on time, and all the guests were already seated in the grounds of the hall when they pulled up. The nerves had finally hit her as her dad offered his arm. He kept muttering gently, 'Breathe, just breathe,' with a steady smile as they made their way towards where Stuart waited for her.

The sun was shining brilliantly, casting a golden hue over the stunning ruins of the hall and its surrounding gardens. The string quartet played softly, their music echoing beautifully around the ancient stone buildings. Their family and friends present, peacocks walking behind the gathering, looking intrigued. Kate could hear the faint ripple of laughter among the guests as she and Stuart shared their non-conventional vows—moments that felt almost dreamlike in their perfection.

Kate chuckled softly to herself as another memory surfaced, one she hadn't thought about in a while. It happened on the drive back to the hotel after the ceremony.

Stuart's dad was driving; her dad sat in the front passenger seat, and Kate and Stuart were tucked in the back. The atmosphere was cheerful and light, the quiet hum of the car soothing—except for one small problem.

'Pull over into that hotel!' Kate suddenly blurted out.

Stuart's dad immediately turned into the hotel and to a gentle halt as she all but leapt out. Desperate, she ran into the hotel reception, her wedding dress trailing behind her, and hurriedly asked the receptionist if she could use the loo.

Moments later, Chloe— her best friend—pulled up in her own car, following Kate straight into the hotel ladies' room. Chloe burst through the door, took one look at Kate, adjusting herself in the mirror, and exclaimed, 'Where the hell have your boobs gone, Kate?'

Kate glanced down at her now suddenly flat chest in the mirror and burst out laughing. It was true: the stress and the lack of food had flattened everything. Chloe, still grinning mischievously, suggested stuffing her bra with toilet paper. The two of them dissolved into fits of giggles as Kate reluctantly followed Chloe's advice, wadding up handfuls of tissue to plump out her bodice.

When they emerged, flushed with laughter, they returned to the hotel reception lobby only to discover that her dad had taken things into his own hands. A large pot of tea and a plate of biscuits were waiting for them on a table.

'Oh, wow, that's so nice! I'm absolutely gasping,' Kate had said, grateful for the gesture.

Her dad turned to her with a wide grin. 'They're just checking the details of your wedding,' he replied nonchalantly.

Kate froze. 'What have you done?' she asked sharply, narrowing her eyes at him.

'Well,' her dad said, looking thoroughly pleased with himself, 'I told them we'd arrived for your wedding reception. Party of 60 are on their way.'

Kate had stared at him, dumbfounded. 'Dad!'

At the time, it hadn't been funny at all. Her face burning, she'd hurried to reception to explain briefly what had happened and that this was her dad's sense of humour whilst apologising profusely on her dad's behalf. The staff had been understanding and gracious about the whole thing, and Kate thanked them sincerely for their unexpected hospitality.

The reception back at the hotel that evening had been nothing short of wonderful. The dinner was relaxed and filled with laughter, the disco buzzing with energy, and the speeches heartfelt. Kate's dad had seized his moment during his speech. With great amusement, he revealed *everything*—the building site, the chaotic morning, the last-minute venue discovery, and even the loo-stop antics.

For all the stress and unexpected twists, the day had turned out to be something extraordinary. The comments poured in throughout the evening—guests marvelling at the stunning venue for the ceremony, asking how on earth they'd found such a beautiful place. Kate had smiled quietly and let her dad do the talking.

Looking back, Kate thought that maybe the chaos was what made it so special. The intimacy of sharing the day with only their closest friends and family had given it a warmth and meaning that no amount of planning could have achieved.

She also remembered that she had told the press photographer to mention why they were having their ceremony at the hall instead of the hotel grounds and to pass on their forever eternal gratitude to the entire Kirby Hall team.

'Kate! Earth to Kate—come in!'

Stuart's voice cut through her reverie, snapping her back to the present. She blinked and turned towards him, a sheepish smile spreading across her face.

'I'm so sorry,' she said with a laugh.

'For some reason, I started to reminisce about our wedding day and all the challenges we faced then,' Kate said softly, more to herself than anyone else.

It surprised her, the clarity with which those memories resurfaced—the laughter, the chaos, the unexpected twists that had turned into cherished moments. Was it just nostalgia or something more? An omen, perhaps? Was this her subconscious trying to tell her something? A warning not to take the risk of leaving for Vietnam?

Jenny's voice broke through her thoughts. 'Well, you'll certainly have many challenges ahead of you both now,' she said with a sad smile.

Kate looked at her mother-in-law and felt a familiar pang of affection mixed with guilt. Jenny was so vibrant and full of life, a woman who seemed to shine in every room she entered. She adored meeting new people, always welcoming everyone with open arms and a kind word. Kate knew she was going to miss her terribly—Jenny's warmth had always been a comfort, her presence a constant in their lives.

'Anyhow, let's not get too sentimental,' Jenny said suddenly, her tone forcibly cheery as she straightened up. 'I asked earlier, what would you like for dinner today? We won't have time tomorrow before we take you to the airport.'

Kate didn't even pause to think. 'Roast lamb, roast potatoes and lots of veggies, please!' she replied with a bright, albeit slightly strained, smile. It was her ultimate comfort meal, the kind that wrapped one in nostalgia and warmth.

Stuart chimed in with his own request, 'Apple and blackberry crumble, custard and cream, please.'

Stuart's mum nodded with a soft smile, already making mental notes for the perfect send-off feast.

That final dinner was both comforting and bittersweet. The table was laden with perfectly roasted lamb, golden potatoes crisped to perfection and an array of colourful vegetables glistening with butter. They laughed and reminisced. The crumble, tart yet sweet, was devoured with an unspoken urgency, as though they could somehow prolong the evening by savouring every bite.

The following day, Kate stumbled through the process of packing her suitcase. Her thoughts were scattered, overwhelmed by the uncertainty of what lay ahead. She ticked off items on her list but kept second-guessing herself: had she packed enough essentials? Was there room for the gifts their families had showered them with?

The phone seemed to ring endlessly. Friends called throughout the day, offering last-minute words of encouragement and affection.

Her heart felt torn. Every smile, every joke, every heartfelt goodbye carved deeper into the conflict within her. Was she leaving behind something, *someone,* more precious than the adventure she had dreamed of since she was a teenager? Was this really worth it?

Sunday, 14th February 1994

In the end, Stuart's mum and dad, along with Kate's mum, couldn't bear the thought of saying goodbye at the airport. The long walk to security, the last hugs, the awkward lingering—none of it seemed manageable. Instead, Liz, ever the dependable and adventurous sister, volunteered to drive Kate and Stuart to the airport.

Jenny hugged Kate tightly before they left, holding on for just a moment longer than usual. 'You'll write. And call,' she whispered.

Her mum hugged Kate tightly and squeezed her hand even tighter. 'See you soon, I promise,' she had said in between genuine sobs and tears running down her cheeks. Both choked with raw emotions and an outpouring of love. 'I love you, Mum, and I am so proud of you. Thank you for believing in me, too,' Kate said as she pulled away.

As they pulled out of the driveway, Kate turned to look back. Stuart's parents and her mum stood huddled together on the doorstep, waving, their faces framed by the fading evening light. It was a bittersweet image that Kate knew would stay with her for a long time.

As they headed to check-in, Stuart's sister, Liz, stopped them. She handed Kate a rather large teddy bear, its soft fur already comforting to the touch. 'For when you need a hug from a friend,' Liz said with a tender smile.

Kate, who had maintained her composure during most of the past three weeks, suddenly broke. She burst into tears and hugged her sister-in-law tightly, as though letting go would shatter her resolve. 'I'll be out to see you before you know it,' Liz promised, her voice filled with certainty as she stepped back towards her car, leaving Kate and Stuart to face the next step of their journey.

At the check-in desk, the queue seemed endless. The mundane chatter with Stuart barely distracted Kate from the heaviness in her chest. Suddenly, she felt a surge of panic.

'I'm going to call Nan and Mum,' Kate blurted out, her words rushed as she turned to find the nearest payphone.

Inside the telephone box, she called her mum. It was a brief conversation, and they were both in tears.

'Mum, you will come out, won't you?'

'I will sort out flights. Just book the time off work.'

'Of course, I will,' she replied before putting down the receiver.

Dialling her Nan's number next, her hands trembling. The voice on the other end was soft and full of love, instantly breaking down Kate's resolve. Her Nan had always been her rock and the person who had said, 'Always write down your dreams.'

Write them down,' her Nan had said when Kate was a teenager. 'No matter how impossible they might seem, write them down, and you'll make them come true.'

From that moment, Kate had kept a Dream Journal, updating it every January with her 'dreams.' As she got older, the dreams/aspirations were split into headings: Career & Business, Financial matters, Social Life & Living, Sport & Wellbeing and Personal Growth, and even Finding Love. Her Nan's belief in her had been unshakable, a guiding light through every twist and turn of her life.

When Kate was old enough to make her own choices, she always found herself sitting by or near the sea. It wasn't just the view—it was the sounds, the salty tang of the air, the rhythm of the waves that seemed to echo the beating of her heart. The sea gave her something she couldn't find anywhere else: space. Space to breathe, to take stock of her life, and to daydream without limits. It was her sanctuary, her *happy place.*

For years, Kate had, besides the absolute desire to travel, nurtured one particular dream—one that carried her through difficult days and restless nights. She imagined herself living in a cosy seaside cottage with a little garden full of colourful wild plants and roses climbing up the walls. It would have a large bedroom filled with soft throws and books stacked on the bedside table, a retreat in itself.

But it was the bathroom she dreamt of most vividly: one large enough to hold one of those enormous corner baths, the kind you could fully stretch out in. She pictured herself sinking into bubbles, a bath that had a space to safely place a glass of wine, candles flickering softly around her, and a book—always a book—within reach.

The cottage would have a couple of spare bedrooms, of course, so her friends and family could stay whenever they wanted. There'd be a cosy living room with a proper log fire, its warmth crackling on winter evenings, flames dancing like magic, mesmerising, hypnotic, enthralling to the eye. But most importantly, the cottage would sit so close to the sea that the scent of seaweed would drift through the open windows, and the salt in the air would cling to her lips. She'd hear the waves gently lapping against the shoreline as she drifted off to sleep and wake to their soothing roar in the mornings.

She dreamt of being able to pull on a jumper, make herself a cup of coffee, and be by the water's edge within two minutes—so close that the sea felt like an extension of her home.

It was a pipe dream, she used to think, shaking her head at herself. And yet, each year, she returned to it. She built the dream a little stronger in her mind, filling in the details, letting it become something tangible—a refuge she could almost touch.

Now, here she was, sobbing her heart out, her shoulders shaking as she spoke to her Nan.

And deep down, even in the middle of her tears, she knew that one day—somehow—she'd find her way to the sea.

'I promise you, Nan,' Kate sobbed into the receiver, 'I'll call you every week. No matter what, I'll come and see you every time I'm back in the UK. I love you so much. Never forget that.'

The finality of the moment overwhelmed her. She slid down the wall of the booth, tears streaming freely as she clung to the receiver, her heart aching with every sob.

A soft tap on the glass startled her. She looked up to see a kind-faced stranger gesturing gently. With effort, Kate pulled herself together, hung up the phone and stepped out, her face flushed with emotion.

Rejoining Stuart in the queue, Kate tried to shake off the lingering sadness. They made small talk to pass the time, but her mind raced. Then, like a lightning strike, panic hit her again.

She frantically patted her coat pockets, then began rummaging through her handbag. Nothing. With a frustrated huff, she tipped the entire contents onto the floor, her hands quivering as she searched.

'What's wrong?' Stuart inquired.

Tears welled in her eyes as she whispered, 'I can't find my Filofax.' Her voice cracked, 'It's got all of our family and friends' telephone numbers and addresses,' she managed between sobs, clutching her bag as if willing the leather-bound organiser to materialise. The weight of its absence hit her hard. That little book was more than a planner; it was her lifeline, especially with everything changing so drastically.

Her sobs grew louder, and Stuart placed a steadying hand on her shoulder. 'Shush,' he said softly, his eyes scanning the surrounding chaos of the airport.

Kate recoiled, her anguish morphing into anger. 'What? Shush? I've lost everything!'

'Shush,' he repeated firmly, holding her gaze. 'Listen.'

Confused, Kate paused, wiping her tear-streaked face as she tried to focus on the sounds around her. Above the din of chatter and luggage wheels rolling on the polished floors, a voice crackled through the PA system:

Would Kate from Oxford please come to the security desk near the BA check-in desk, Zone C? We have an item of yours.'

Kate froze for a moment, then turned to Stuart.

'Thank God,' she breathed, her voice trembling.

As they hurried towards the security desk, Kate muttered, half to herself, 'Talk about leaving your brain at home.' The ridiculousness of it all caught up with them, and they both laughed, their relief bubbling over in shared amusement.

At the security desk, a kindly man in a uniform held up her Filofax with a knowing smile. 'This must be yours?'

Kate nearly snatched it from him in her eagerness, clutching it to her chest as though it were a missing child. 'Thank you so much,' she gushed, her voice thick with emotion. 'You don't know how grateful I am. This Filofax is my most treasured possession. It'll be my saviour when we're in Vietnam.'

The man chuckled, clearly amused by her heartfelt gratitude, and waved them off with a good-natured, 'Safe travels!'

With her Filofax safely back in her possession, Kate finally began to breathe a little easier. Still, her nerves felt frayed, and she was emotionally drained by the time they boarded their flight.

Their first destination was Bangkok, a two-night stopover to meet with the company's joint venture partner in Thailand. This partner had been instrumental in helping them secure a key contact in Vietnam to establish a similar partnership there—a crucial step in how business was conducted in the region.

Kate leaned back in her seat as the plane taxied for take-off. She gazed out of the window, the English winter fading away beneath her. In her mind, she tried to picture Bangkok, the sprawling metropolis she'd only transited through in the past, not venturing out of the airport. She realized, with a twinge of guilt, that she hadn't researched Thailand or Vietnam at all. The last three weeks had been a whirlwind of long hours at work handing over, packing, goodbyes, and last-minute preparations, leaving no time for even a cursory investigation or search.

What she did know came from snippets of conversation, vague recollections and what was written on the government websites: Bangkok, or *Krung Thep Maha Nakhon* as it was locally known, was renowned for its tropical climate. February would be hot and humid, with daytime temperatures ranging between 23 and 32 degrees Celsius. She imagined bustling streets filled with tuk-tuks, markets overflowing with vibrant produce and ornate temples glinting under the sun.

Beyond that, Vietnam remained an enigma. Luckily, she had picked up a guidebook from the travel agent and tossed it in her bag, hoping to skim through it on her way to Bangkok.

Finally, having just enough time to familiarize herself with the history of Vietnam, Kate began reading the book. She had been advised that it would be prudent to have at least a basic understanding of the country's political and cultural history, as well as its social expectations, before her arrival.

The book explained that the region around present-day Hanoi had been settled in prehistoric times and was often chosen as a political centre by Chinese conquerors. In 1010, Ly Thai To, the first ruler of the Ly dynasty (1009–1225), designated the site of Hanoi—then known as Thang Long, meaning 'Rising Dragon'—as his capital. Thang Long remained Vietnam's capital until 1802 when the Nguyen dynasty (1802–1945) moved the capital south to Hue. Over time, the city underwent several name changes. One of these, Dong Kinh, bestowed during the later Le dynasty (1428–1787), was corrupted by Europeans into 'Tonquin.' During the French colonial period (1883–1945), Tonkin referred to the entire northern region.

In 1831, the Nguyen dynasty renamed the city Ha Noi, which translates to 'Between Two Rivers.' Under French rule, Hanoi became an administrative hub, and in 1902, it was declared the capital of French Indochina. This decision was influenced by the region's proximity to southern China, where the French sought to expand their influence, as well as its rich mineral resources. Hanoi remained a key administrative centre during the Japanese occupation (1940–1945).

In August 1945, following Japan's surrender, the Viet Minh, led by Ho Chi Minh, seized power in Hanoi, declaring it the capital of the Democratic Republic of Vietnam. However, French forces reasserted control from 1946 until their decisive defeat at Dien Bien Phu in 1954. Thereafter, Hanoi resumed its status as the capital of North Vietnam.

The city endured heavy bombing by the United States in 1965, 1968 and 1972, suffering massive destruction. After the fall of Saigon on 30th April 1975, North Vietnam consolidated control over the entire country. On 2nd July 1976, the Socialist Republic of Vietnam was officially established, with Hanoi as its enduring capital.

Since 1954, Hanoi has transformed from a primarily commercial city into an industrial and agricultural hub. Key industries include the production of machine tools, electric generators, plywood, textiles, chemicals and matches. The surrounding area supports agriculture, producing rice, fruits, vegetables, cereals and industrial crops.

Hanoi is also a major communications centre. Its roads link it to other Vietnamese cities, and railway lines connect it to Haiphong's port, Kunming in China's Yunnan province, and Ho Chi Minh City (formerly Saigon). Small oceangoing vessels navigate the Red River to Hanoi, while numerous smaller rivers facilitate trade across northern Vietnam.

Despite centuries of war and foreign aggression, Hanoi retains several historical and scenic landmarks. These include Hoan Kiem Lake ('Lake of the Restored Sword'), the Co Loa Citadel from the 3rd century BCE, the Temple of Literature (dedicated to Confucius in 1070), the One-Pillar Pagoda (1049) and the Temple of the Trung Sisters (1142). The Imperial Citadel of Thang Long, built in the 11th century, remains a key historical site. Cultural institutions such as the University of Hanoi, the Revolutionary Museum, the Army Museum and the National Museum further enrich the city.

As Kate read through the first few chapters, she couldn't help but wonder if she'd even be allowed into the country, let alone permitted to work there. It all seemed so far removed from what she knew—almost as though Vietnam was still trapped in the dark ages, at least 40 years behind the UK. The human rights issues, communist ideologies and rigid practices still in place were daunting. How on earth was she going to live and work under such restrictions?

Eleven and a half hours on a flight proved to be far more pleasant than Kate had anticipated. From the moment they settled into their seats, the attentive cabin crew ensured they were well looked after. Sparkling wine, spirits, beers and snacks seemed to appear endlessly, and wine was served with their dinner. Breakfast the next morning came accompanied by warm flannels to refresh them before landing. The overnight flight, though long, allowed for a few hours of decent sleep, and Kate found herself relatively rested when they touched down in Bangkok.

It was an unforgettable experience spending Valentine's Day 33,000 feet above the ground. Romantic? Not quite. The cabin was packed to capacity, and while the idea of celebrating in the skies sounded charming, the reality involved clinking plastic glasses amidst the chatter of dozens of other passengers. Still, the novelty of the occasion brought a smile to Kate's face.

Chapter 5: Tuk Tuks and Temples

*A*s they disembarked the plane, the thick, humid air of Thailand wrapped around them like a sticky blanket. Kate, dressed in her cosy travel attire of a sweatshirt, tracksuit bottoms, and trainers, felt instantly overdressed. A rivulet of sweat trickled down her back, and beads began forming on her forehead. She grimaced, suddenly hyper-aware of how she must smell after the long flight. The sensation triggered an unwelcome memory of the meeting with George, where she'd felt similarly clammy and self-conscious.

Kate wiped her brow discreetly as they were ushered toward the baggage claim area. The vehicle transporting them was a rickety old bus that looked as though it had been plucked straight out of the 1940s. Its charm lay in its antiquity, but Kate couldn't help but laugh at the juxtaposition of their modern plane and this vintage ride.

Thankfully, their luggage arrived intact, and with passports stamped at customs, they headed outside to hail a taxi.

The roads of Bangkok were like nothing Kate had ever seen. What she had initially thought might be slightly better than dirt tracks turned out to be a chaotic maze of traffic, blaring horns, and what appeared to be a complete absence of road rules. Vehicles darted between lanes without warning, scooters weaved dangerously close to cars, and the concept of orderly driving seemed nonexistent.

Adding to the chaos was the pollution. The smog hung low over the city like an oppressive fog, reducing visibility to barely fifty feet. In hindsight, Kate thought, perhaps it was a blessing. If she could have seen further, she might have been even more alarmed by the mayhem unfolding on the roads.

Their hotel, a serene oasis amid the bustling city, was a welcome reprieve. After the sweaty taxi ride, Kate wasted no time hopping into the shower, relishing the feeling of cool water washing away the grime and tension of travel. Once refreshed, they joined their Thai joint venture partner for brunch, a meal filled with introductions, warm smiles, and discussions of the business connections they were set to build.

With the formalities complete, Kate and Stuart decided to seize the day. Bangkok was a city brimming with history and culture, and the Grand Palace was at the top of their list.

The Grand Palace exceeded every expectation. A sprawling complex of gilded temples, intricately detailed stupas and dazzling architecture, it left Kate utterly spellbound. The main courtyard was a symphony of colour and light, with every surface glinting in the golden sunlight. Compared to the stately but subdued elegance of Buckingham Palace, the Grand Palace felt like stepping into another world—one where opulence reigned supreme.

Kate wandered the grounds in awe, her gaze drawn to every shimmering detail. There were bejewelled mythological creatures guarding temple entrances, their forms both fantastical and fearsome. The temple roofs, inverted and ornate, gleamed in hues of emerald and sapphire, their craftsmanship so intricate that Kate could hardly fathom how such beauty was even possible.

'I can't believe this exists,' she murmured to Stuart, her voice hushed with reverence.

'It's incredible,' he agreed, equally entranced.

Every corner of the palace seemed to hold a new wonder. Kate found herself lingering by a particular stupa adorned with golden tiles that sparkled like a cascade of light. The richness and attention to detail were overwhelming, and for a moment, she felt an almost spiritual connection to the artistry surrounding her.

After a few hours surrounded by the dazzling beauty of the Grand Palace, Kate and Stuart decided to take their exploration further. They hailed a *Tuk Tuk*, the quirky three-wheeled vehicle that buzzed noisily through Bangkok's chaotic streets. With its tiny petrol engine and flimsy canopy roof that barely offered shade, the *Tuk Tuk* seemed both exhilarating and precarious.

The hotel concierge had suggested a visit to Chinatown, where a special celebration was taking place. 'It'll be magical to see,' he'd promised, his smile filled with enthusiasm.

Kate and Stuart clambered into the back of the *Tuk Tuk*, gripping the sides tightly as the driver navigated through the thrumming streets. Bangkok's traffic was as wild as ever, but the novelty of the ride filled them with excitement.

As they arrived in Chinatown, it was clear the celebration had quietened for the day. Most of the shops were shuttered, their signs hanging forlornly in the humid air. Only a few street vendors remained, their colourful wares displayed beneath bright umbrellas. Stalls laden with vibrant fruits, bundles of flowers, and neatly arranged incense sticks created a striking contrast to the empty streets around them. Lanterns swayed gently overhead, casting soft glows of red and gold in the dimming light.

'Not quite the magical celebration we were promised,' Stuart remarked.

The *Tuk Tuk* driver, noticing their unease, perked up and gestured energetically toward a nearby temple. Its grand entrance was adorned with intricately carved Chinese dragons, their sinuous bodies draped elegantly on either side of the towering gate.

'Go! Go!' he urged, beckoning them to explore.

Kate hesitated for a moment, then turned to the driver. 'Will you wait for us?' she asked, miming the action as best she could.

The driver nodded vigorously, his grin reassuring.

The temple courtyard was a sight that took their breath away. Dominating the centre were three enormous golden statues of the Buddha, their serene expressions radiating a quiet majesty. The golden figures glowed softly under the lantern-lit sky, creating an ethereal aura that seemed to hum with reverence.

Hundreds of monks in saffron robes knelt before the statues, their heads bowed in unison. Their chanting filled the courtyard with a rhythmic, hypnotic melody, rising and falling in perfect harmony. Each monk held an incense stick aloft, its thin plume of smoke curling skyward. The air was thick with the rich, heady scent of incense, its intensity making Kate feel slightly dizzy.

'It's unbelievable,' she whispered to Stuart, her voice barely audible.

He nodded silently, his gaze fixed on the scene before them.

For a few moments, they simply stood there, enveloped in the tranquil beauty of the moment. It was unlike anything Kate had ever experienced, a profound stillness that felt worlds away from the bustling streets they had just left behind.

Eventually, they tore themselves away, walking softly back through the temple gates. True to his word, their *Tuk Tuk* driver was waiting patiently, his smile unchanged.

'What a gem,' Stuart said, slipping a generous tip into the man's hand as they climbed into the vehicle.

'Can you come back tomorrow morning?' he added, making sure the arrangement was clear. The driver nodded enthusiastically before whisking them back to their hotel through the now dimly lit streets.

The next day was a flurry of meetings at the offices of their joint venture partner. It was an intense session of information gathering, with Kate and Stuart pouring over stacks of documents. They absorbed as much as they could about setting up a partnership in Vietnam, including trading laws, import/export systems, and the intricate details of local business practices.

'Do you think it's possible to adapt some of the systems here for Vietnam?' Kate asked Stuart during a short break.

'It's going to take work,' he replied, running a hand through his hair. 'But it's a good starting point.'

They also gleaned valuable insights into the Western companies already operating in Vietnam and compiled a comprehensive list of embassy contacts. By the end of the day, they felt both overwhelmed and optimistic.

That afternoon, their *Tuk Tuk* driver returned, ready to show them more of Bangkok. This time, Kate had learned an important survival tip: never look down or behind. The chaotic flow of traffic, with its erratic movements and apparent lack of rules, was enough to unsettle even the steadiest nerves.

'Just keep looking straight ahead,' she joked to Stuart as they held on tightly. 'Otherwise, you'll want to jump off before we crash!'

Stuart laughed, though his knuckles were white from gripping the seat.

The evening arrived, and their Thai hosts treated them to an unforgettable cultural experience. The setting was a stunning open-air venue illuminated by the warm glow of lanterns. Performers took to the stage in elaborate traditional costumes, their movements a graceful dance of storytelling and artistry.

Dinner was served in a series of beautifully presented dishes, each bursting with the vibrant flavours of Thai cuisine. There were spicy curries, fragrant jasmine rice, and an array of delicacies infused with lemongrass, chilli and coconut.

Kate savoured every bite, marvelling at the richness of the flavours. As she sat back, watching the dancers move in synchronized harmony, she felt a rare sense of contentment.

Chapter 6: A Taste of Vietnam

The following morning, Kate and Stuart were taken to the airport to board a flight to Hanoi.

Flying with the Russian airline Aeroflot from Bangkok to Hanoi was an experience unlike any other. There were no seat allocations at check-in, and luggage was left untagged. A creaky 1940s-era bus ferried passengers from the terminal to the plane. Among the passengers was a Vietnamese man carrying a basket with six live ducks, another with a crate of a dozen hens and several others clutching baskets of plants and fruit. The scene felt like something straight out of a film.

Kate and Stuart managed to find two seats together and buckled themselves in, bracing for what promised to be a memorable flight. The safety demonstration was so brief it barely registered, and the take-off was utterly terrifying. The engines whined loudly, and the wings flexed alarmingly as the plane taxied along the runway. For a moment, as the aircraft struggled to gain speed, Kate felt certain it wouldn't lift off. She clutched the armrest tightly, her stomach twisting with apprehension. Somehow, against all odds, the plane ascended, leaving Bangkok behind and carrying them towards an uncertain future in Hanoi.

Quacking ducks, clucking hens and a Vietnamese gentleman seated next to Kate noisily slurping his noodles—splashing consommé in every direction—made for an unforgettable flight. The chaotic tableau, while slightly comical, served as a welcome distraction from the unnerving, fluctuating noises emanating from the plane's engines. The aircraft seemed to climb and descend erratically, prompting

Kate to convince herself it was merely turbulence. Her grip on Stuart's hand tightened unconsciously, her nails digging into his skin.

The engines, instead of emitting their usual steady hum, growled and surged unpredictably.

'We'll be fine,' Stuart said calmly, his voice assuring amidst the disconcerting cacophony.

'Really? I don't feel fine at the moment,' Kate replied, hastily withdrawing her hand. 'Sorry for clawing you. It wasn't intentional,' she added with a sheepish smile.

Kate attempted to distract herself by discreetly observing the Vietnamese gentleman beside her. Fascinated by his methodical approach to eating noodles, she watched as he deftly manoeuvred his chopsticks, lifting a portion of noodles halfway out of the consommé. The noodles dangled mid-air as he tilted his face towards them, noisily sucking each strand into his mouth with remarkable precision. He repeated this ritualized action until the bowl was empty, following it with an audible slurp of the remaining soup directly from the bowl.

Thankfully, Kate had practised using chopsticks for two weeks before leaving the UK, anticipating that it might demonstrate a measure of respect for Vietnamese customs. Even so, she found the noodles rather bland and overwhelmingly salty, leaving her parched. She quenched her thirst with several cups of green tea, which she found vastly preferable to the thick, tar-like coffee Stuart had opted for.

Seeking further distraction, Kate opened her book to learn more about the country that would be her home for at least the next two years. With over an hour left on the flight, she immersed herself in its pages.

The text detailed the Red River, or Song Hong, the principal river of northern Vietnam. Originating in central Yunnan province in southwestern China, it flows southeast through a deep gorge across the Tonkin region, passing through Hanoi before emptying into the Gulf of Tonkin. Spanning nearly 750 miles, the river's flow is bolstered by two major tributaries: the Song Lo (Clear River) on the left bank and the Song Da (Black River) on the right. During the rainy season, the river's flow can surge to an astonishing 335,500 cubic feet per second. Its volume fluctuates dramatically throughout the year, and it carries vast quantities of silt due to the crumbly soil in its basin. This distinctive red soil lends the river its name.

The sediment is deposited in the Red River Delta, a flat triangular region covering about 2,700 square miles, stretching 93 miles inland and 50 miles along the coast. Densely populated and intensively farmed, the delta forms a crucial part of northern Vietnam. Haiphong, located on the northern arm of the delta, serves as Hanoi's outport.

Closing the book with a sigh, Kate wondered aloud about their imminent landing in Hanoi.

'What do you think it'll be like?' she asked Stuart.

'It'll be fine,' he replied without looking up from his own book, his tone maddeningly composed.

Kate envied his calmness. If only she could adopt his nonchalant outlook, life would be far less stressful, she mused, gazing out of the window.

As it turned out, the landing was every bit as dramatic as she had feared. The plane bounced roughly upon touching the runway, throwing passengers and belongings into disarray. Pandemonium ensued well before the aircraft came to a halt. Passengers leapt from their seats, jostling for position in the aisle despite the lack of any announcement or instruction to remain seated.

Boxes, baskets and bags tumbled from overhead compartments, spilling their contents. A man carrying a basket of ducks pushed his way through the chaos, the basket swinging precariously above people's heads. Kate winced as she imagined the poor ducks being jostled and squashed amidst the commotion.

Stuart, ever pragmatic, suggested they remain seated until the rush subsided. 'We're not in a hurry, after all,' he said. Kate nodded in agreement, leaning into him for a brief moment of comfort.

When they finally disembarked, the sweltering heat and humidity hit them with the same ferocity as it had in Bangkok. Kate was grateful for the linen dress she had purchased during their stopover, which provided some relief in the oppressive climate. Still, beads of perspiration quickly formed on her back and began trickling down her cleavage.

As they stepped into the chaos of Hanoi, Kate realised this was just the beginning of what promised to be a challenging yet fascinating chapter of her life.

As they looked down the steps, their luggage lay scattered across the landing strip, abandoned in a haphazard array. Each of them picked up two suitcases, the humid air already clinging to their skin, and started making their way towards what they assumed was the arrivals terminal. There was no carousel, no luggage trolleys, and certainly no air-conditioned hall to greet them—just the oppressive heat and the faint scent of jet fuel lingering in the air.

'Hi there, you must be Kate and Stuart?' came a cheerful voice as a tall, solidly built man approached. 'I'm Ken, from the British Embassy—locally employed, no diplomatic status for me,' he added with a self-deprecating chuckle, as though embarrassed by the distinction.

Ken was around 6'2", dressed in casual beige linen trousers, an open-collared shirt and a pair of open-toed sandals. He exuded a sense of relaxed authority, his easy manner a welcome contrast to the chaos surrounding them.

Without waiting for a response, Ken grabbed Kate's suitcases and gestured for them to follow. 'Stick close and keep quiet unless spoken to by customs officials. It's just easier that way—especially for you, Kate,' he said, glancing at her.

Kate frowned. 'Oh? Why's that?'

'Shush, will you?' Stuart interjected.

They walked in silence, the hum of the runway replaced by the faint rustle of feathers and murmurs of the remaining staff. Everyone else from the plane had already dispersed, leaving only a few stray hen feathers behind as a reminder of their unusual flight.

Ahead, six men in dark green uniforms marched towards them, their caps pulled so low it was difficult to see their eyes. Each carried a rifle slung over a shoulder. The sight struck Kate as more military than civilian—definitely not the friendly image of a local bobby she was accustomed to.

'You, come here!' barked one of the men, pointing directly at Kate.

Her stomach tightened. She bit her lip, clenching her fists instinctively, and glanced at Stuart, who gave her a subtle nod to comply. Ken, standing slightly to her side, met her gaze and offered the same silent encouragement.

Taking a deep breath, Kate stepped forward cautiously.

'Passport!' the man demanded.

Kate fumbled to retrieve it, her hands trembling as she handed it over.

'You English? From Oxford?' he asked, his voice loud, almost accusatory.

'Yes,' Kate replied, biting her lip and forcing herself to maintain eye contact.

'Good! You teach all police and generals English!' he barked.

'What? But I'm not a teacher. I'm here for work,' Kate stammered, her voice shaking.

'You teach us English!' he repeated, louder this time, raising his hand as though to emphasize the point.

Ken stepped forward quickly and whispered, 'Vietnamese army—just do as they say, Kate. You're one of only a handful of Western women to come here to work and certainly the only one in your line of business. It's best to go with the flow.'

Tears pricked her eyes as she nodded, staring at the ground. Her heart pounded as she struggled to hold back the sobs building in her chest. She felt Stuart's hand reach for hers, offering a reassuring squeeze, but it did little to quell the rising panic.

The officer signalled them to follow, leading them to a minibus parked in front of the airport entrance. They bypassed customs entirely—no inspections, no questions.

As the officer opened the door, he motioned for Kate to get in. Stuart moved to follow, but the officer raised his hand abruptly.

'No! Just her,' he growled.

'No way,' Stuart said firmly, though his voice remained quiet. 'Where Kate goes, I go.'

Ken intervened, speaking to the officer in what sounded to Kate like fluent Vietnamese. After a brief exchange, Ken turned to them. 'It's fine. We can all get in together,' he said calmly.

'Thank you,' Kate murmured, her voice thick with emotion as she climbed into the minibus. She took a deep breath, staring out of the window. *What on earth have we done?* she thought as the vehicle jolted forward.

The ride to central Hanoi was rough and uncomfortable. The 'road' was more of a dirt track, riddled with potholes that sent the 'minibus' (more like a converted army truck) bouncing violently. Dust rose in thick clouds, obscuring much of the view, reminiscent of the smog she had seen in Bangkok. Through the haze, she caught glimpses of the Mekong River, wider than she had imagined, its waters lapping precariously close to the top of what Kate thought was a very low retaining wall that would not offer any protection from the increasing highwater levels and strong flow of the river.

She noticed men and women labouring along the riverbank, stacking stones and blocks onto the wall, filling gaps with what appeared to be a mixture of straw and manure. The process seemed futile to Kate—surely the makeshift cement wouldn't set before the rising water washed it all away. *Do they really repeat this every year? What a waste of time, energy and resources,* she thought.

The minibus came to an abrupt halt. Ahead, a buffalo stood motionless in the middle of the road, its owner struggling in vain to coax it aside. An army officer got out to assist, and together, they managed to drag the stubborn animal to the verge.

As they continued, Kate observed women along the roadside, most dressed in black or dark brown outfits with conical hats shielding their faces, only their eyes visible. Many carried heavy baskets filled with stones or straw, likely for the men building the wall. The scene underscored the region's vulnerability to the annual floods she had read about. Why hadn't the government invested in lasting flood defences?

Finally, the minibus pulled up outside what Ken described as their hotel. To Kate, it looked more like a private house— narrow, perhaps only eight feet wide, and three storeys tall. Its modest façade featured a single window on each floor, and the entrance was so small that both Stuart and Ken had to duck to get inside.

'Kate and Stuart, you'll drop your luggage here, then we'll head to the General's office. I'll stay with you,' Ken explained.

'Okay,' Stuart replied. Kate remained silent, still processing the surreal events of the day.

The next moment, the officer grabbed Kate by the arm, pulling her out of the minibus with startling force.

'This way. You,'—he pointed to Stuart—'stay here. You,' pointing to Ken, 'come with her,' he commanded in Vietnamese. Ken nodded, translating the instructions when necessary.

Five flights of stairs later, they arrived in a stifling room without a door, the window openings barren of glass. A large blackboard dominated the front wall, and a ceiling fan hung motionless, seemingly out of service. Kate, panting from the climb, was drenched in sweat, her hair clinging in limp strands around her face. Dust clung stubbornly to her arms and face, sticking to the sheen of perspiration. Though Kate was not one to fuss over her appearance, she at least liked to feel clean and presentable—something she decidedly was not at that moment.

Suddenly, the rhythmic sound of marching boots echoed up the stairwell. The cadence was precise, almost musical, and for a brief moment, Kate found the synchrony oddly enchanting. But the enchantment quickly gave way to unease as the sound grew louder. Over thirty army officers, all clad in crisp uniforms, marched into the room and lined up with military precision.

Kate instinctively stepped back, pressing herself closer to the blackboard, where Ken joined her.

'What's going on?' she whispered, panicked.

Ken glanced at her, equally uncertain. 'I think this is your first group to teach English,' he said, his voice laced with disbelief.

'I want Stuart here. Now,' Kate demanded, growing evidently uneasy.

'Hold on. I'll see what I can do,' Ken replied, leaving her alone in the room with over thirty stoic officers staring at her in unnerving silence.

A moment later, Stuart entered alongside Ken, followed by an authoritative man whom Kate quickly recognised as the Army General.

'You teach us English now. And every night,' the General commanded, his tone leaving no room for negotiation.

Kate turned to Ken, her voice trembling. 'Tell him I'm not an English teacher. I've never taught anyone anything. I don't even know how to teach English, let alone every night. I'm here to work for a company, not teach.'

Ken hesitated before translating, his expression neutral. The General listened impassively before replying in curt Vietnamese.

Ken sighed. 'He's agreed that you'll teach every other night for two hours after your regular work. Starting tonight.'

'But…' Kate began, only for Ken to cut her off.

'No buts, Kate. You don't have a choice. This is a Communist country, and you're a Western woman. If you don't comply, you'll likely be deported—or worse, imprisoned. At least he's agreed that Stuart can stay with you tonight.'

Kate's frustration bubbled over. 'How am I supposed to teach them? I don't speak a word of Vietnamese. I'm a woman; they're all men—how is this ever going to work?'

Ken offered a reassuring smile. 'Don't worry. I'll help you translate tonight. Let's figure out the rest as we go. Also, I'll find some chalk.'

'Thank you,' Kate said, her voice softening slightly.

Turning to the group, she began. 'Good evening,' she said hesitantly.

Ken translated. 'Chào buổi tối.'

'My name is Kate. I'm pleased to meet you all.'

Again, Ken translated. 'Tên tôi là Kate. Tôi rất vui được gặp tất cả các bạn.'

The next two hours were a whirlwind. With Ken's invaluable help, Kate managed to piece together a rudimentary lesson, teaching basic English phrases and responses. The officers, though stern and silent, appeared to engage with the material.

When the lesson ended, the General commanded the officers to leave. As they filed out, each one bowed their head respectfully as they passed Kate.

Before the General exited, Kate turned to Ken. 'Can you ask him to provide chairs for the officers? It might help them concentrate during the lessons.'

Ken raised an eyebrow at the request but translated nonetheless. To Kate's surprise, the General agreed, even asking Ken to convey his gratitude to her.

As the door closed behind the General, Kate let out a shaky breath. 'Thank you, Ken. I couldn't have done this without you. Can we at least buy you and your wife a drink as a small thank-you?'

Ken laughed heartily. 'You won't find a pub anywhere in Hanoi. But come back to the Embassy compound. Anne has already prepared dinner, and we've got drinks waiting. There's a spare room and shower for you both if you'd like to stay the night.'

'That sounds amazing. Can we, Stuart?' Kate asked, relieved.

'Absolutely,' Stuart replied.

They left the building together, making their way through the dimly lit streets. The air was thick and still, alive with the hum of mosquitoes that seemed to target Kate exclusively. Dust swirled around them, kicked up by bicycles and motorbikes weaving through the crowds. Street vendors sat on low stools, their goods displayed in baskets or on makeshift tables.

'The mosquitoes love you, Kate,' Ken said with a grin. 'A few glasses of red wine should help. It's a natural antihistamine.'

'Bang me, bang me, bang me!' (bánh mỳ)

Kate turned to Ken, wide-eyed. 'What on earth is she selling? That sounds… rude.'

Ken laughed. 'It's bread—like small French loaves.'

Kate and Stuart burst into laughter. 'First day, first Vietnamese words learned: "Bang me!"' Kate said, giggling.

When they arrived at the Embassy compound, Ken introduced them to the guard before leading them to his home. A lush courtyard greeted them, filled with the calming scent of lavender and the vibrant colours of orange blossoms illuminated by soft lighting. Kate inhaled deeply, revelling in the tranquillity after the chaos of the day.

Anne greeted them with open arms. 'Welcome to Hanoi! Would you like a glass of bubbly or red wine while you freshen up? I've also left a few shift dresses on the bed in case you'd like to borrow one,' she said warmly.

Kate, overwhelmed by her kindness, smiled. 'A glass of red would be lovely. Thank you so much, Anne. And Ken mentioned it's good for mosquito bites—I'm certainly going to need it!'

As she showered, Kate reflected on the day. The warm water washed away the grime and tension, and by the time she emerged, she felt like a new person. The dresses Anne had laid out fitted perfectly despite her petite frame. Kate chose a bright red shift dress, marvelling at how thoughtful her hosts were.

Breathe in, breathe out. Breathe in, breathe out. Relax, Kate told herself as she walked downstairs.

Downstairs, Stuart was chatting with Ken over a beer, and for the first time that day, Kate felt a sense of ease.

The evening was a balm for the day's chaos—relaxed, welcoming and immense relief. Anne and Ken were the perfect hosts, ensuring Kate and Stuart felt at ease. The meal was a sumptuous three-course affair, a celebration of Vietnamese cuisine, complemented by generous servings of red wine and beer. As they ate, Ken and Anne shared a wealth of experiences and invaluable advice about living and working in Vietnam.

'You should expect to be followed around the clock,' Anne explained, her tone serious. 'Any faxes or telephone calls you send or receive will be diverted and vetted by the government, especially as you're a woman working in import and export. It's just how it is here.'

Kate's eyes widened, her anxiety bubbling to the surface. 'Followed? And vetted? Constantly?'

Anne nodded. 'Yes, and I'd also recommend advising your clients not to bring photo albums, books, personal papers, videos, or magazines. The officials will likely confiscate them, and they might even be destroyed. They see all Western papers, magazines, pictures, etc., as propaganda and negative influence.

Kate turned to Stuart, her voice filled with regret. 'Oh, Stuart, I'm so sorry. I was so insistent on bringing all our photo albums and books. I just wanted something from home, something of our family with us. If I'd known, I'd never have brought them. I just hope customs are kind to us.'

Ken interjected with a wry smile. 'You might also want to acquire a taste for whisky—both of you. It'll help when dealing with the customs officials. And be prepared to offer what's known here as "tea money." It's a necessary part of doing business in Vietnam.'

'Tea money?' Kate asked, puzzled.

'A polite way of saying "bribe money,"' Ken clarified. 'For now, it's the norm. For example, it's about $500 USD for a 20-foot container and $1,000 USD for a 40-foot container. Airfreight depends on the volume.'

Stuart sighed but nodded. 'I suppose we'll just have to accept it's part of the system here.'

Kate leaned back in her chair, her mind already spinning with the enormity of their new responsibilities. 'We have so much to do before we can even think about shipments—recruiting operational and office staff, establishing a solid relationship with the Vietnamese partner for the joint venture, developing and expanding the office and getting to grips with all the documentation. At least we don't have any shipments arriving just yet.'

Ken chuckled softly, clearly amused. 'Actually, there are four 40-foot containers arriving in three weeks—for the Australian Embassy. They're building a new embassy here in Hanoi, and the shipment includes machinery, equipment and four vehicles. I've already let them know you're setting up a relocation office, and I can introduce you to their project manager. He's Scottish, and his accent is still as thick as ever despite having lived abroad for over two decades.'

Kate beamed, her earlier worry momentarily replaced by excitement. 'Ken, that's amazing! Thank you for trusting us before we've even started. What a fantastic opportunity.'

'It's a good start,' Stuart agreed, raising his glass in a toast.

They discussed the informal setup of the company's current representation in Vietnam—a small, relaxed operation with a reliable Filipino gentleman managing the office and a few Vietnamese staff handling the warehouse. It was clear there was plenty of room for growth, and both Kate and Stuart felt the weight of the challenge ahead.

As the evening wound down, Stuart rose from his seat. 'I think we should get some sleep. It sounds like we're going to be flat out from now on. Anne, Ken, thank you both so much for making us feel so welcome, and Ken, your help today was beyond anything we could have hoped for. If there's ever anything we can do for you, please let us know.'

'Deal,' Ken replied, shaking Stuart's hand firmly.

Anne embraced them both warmly. 'Goodnight, you two. Sleep well.'

Back in their room, Kate closed the door and immediately hugged Stuart tightly. She felt an overwhelming sense of gratitude that she wasn't facing this alone. Despite her fears, a small glimmer of hope flickered—maybe things would work out after all.

'I have no idea how I'm going to structure these English lessons or even where to begin with the business, but it's only the first day. No need to panic,' Kate said, half to herself.

Stuart returned her embrace and sighed. 'I feel okay about being here, but let's take it one day at a time. No high expectations for the first few months, yeah?'

Kate nodded.

'I'm not thrilled about being followed and spied on—having our calls and faxes monitored. But I suppose I'll have to find a way to live with it,' Stuart added.

Kate looked up at him, her resolve strengthening. 'We'll figure it out together. One step at a time.'

With that, they both lay down, their weary eyes teetering on the edge of surrender. The ceiling fan above them swirled steadily, its gentle breeze a welcome reprieve from the oppressive humidity. Kate's gaze drifted to the window frame, where a small gecko clung motionless. A faint smile touched her lips as she silently resolved that wherever they made their home, geckoes would be a must—they loved mosquitos, after all.

To her relief, the bed was surprisingly soft, the cotton sheets fresh and crisp against her skin. Her head sank into the plump pillows, their embrace almost decadent after the day's chaos. With a long, gentle exhale, she let the tension slip away, her mind giving in to exhaustion.

As sleep took her, a thought danced in her mind, bringing a faint smile to her lips: *Dare to venture into the unknown.* She and Stuart certainly had.

Chapter 7: Through the Chaos – A Cup of Tea

The following day, Kate awoke before sunrise. She decided to wear the red shift dress and venture out to explore the local food market. Anne had mentioned it was only a few minutes' walk from the Embassy compound, assuring her she couldn't possibly get lost. Little did Anne know that Kate's sense of direction was practically nonexistent.

Within half an hour, Kate was regretting her choice of attire. The oppressive humidity had left her dress clinging uncomfortably to her skin, soaked through with sweat. As she made her way through the lively market, she became acutely aware of her shoes filling with muddy water, the unpleasant squelch of mud rising between her toes with every step.

The market was alive with sounds and smells

'Snort, snort, snort, sniff, sniff.'

'Cluck, cluck, cluck, quack, quack.'

'Bang me, bang me, bang me!' cried a woman.

Kate froze momentarily, startled, until she realised the woman was selling bread. Laughing to herself, she muttered, 'Oh, of course—"bánh mì."'

Suddenly, the chaotic harmony of the market was shattered.

'Beep beep!'

'Aaaaarghh!'
Screech. Crash.

Kate turned abruptly to see a woman sprawled sideways on the market floor, her small Vespa lying on top of her. The engine roared loudly, her right hand still gripping the throttle, and the front wheel spun furiously in the air. Kate's heart pounded as she pushed through the throng of onlookers to help.

But to her dismay, no one else seemed remotely concerned about the woman. Instead, the crowd surged towards the Vespa, ignoring the injured lady entirely. As Kate struggled through the pressing bodies, she realised they weren't just ignoring her—they were actively taking away the produce from her baskets. Women of all ages and sizes clambered over the fallen Vespa, clawing at the white hessian bags hanging from the handlebars and pannier baskets. Some tore at the strings with sharp stones or blades; others resorted to biting the knots open with their teeth.

Kate was appalled. The elderly woman lay terrified amidst the chaos, completely overlooked.

Kate's attempt to intervene was interrupted when her foot slipped, sending her sprawling onto the filthy ground. Her hands landed in a rancid puddle of water mixed with sewage. As she pushed herself up, she noticed the market floor littered with dried mushrooms, trampled underfoot in the frenzy.

'Seriously? Mushrooms?' Kate thought, incredulous. Was this what had driven the crowd into such a frenzy? Why were they so desperate for these?

She brushed her muddy hands on the hem of her dress—there was no choice. Tissues and wet wipes weren't exactly commonplace in Vietnam.

By the time she managed to stand, most of the crowd had disappeared, along with the mushrooms. The elderly woman was still there, visibly shaken but clinging to her Vespa. Kate carefully helped her up, noticing how frail she felt under her touch. The woman's back was hunched, her movements slow.

The old woman gave Kate a warm smile, her teeth blackened and stained red from chewing sugar beet or tobacco leaves. As she steadied herself, a sudden hubbub erupted again. Four tiny ducklings had escaped from the crushed front basket of the Vespa, causing another scramble among the remaining market-goers. Kate managed to catch two of them and handed them back to the woman, who nodded in gratitude before disappearing into the crowd.

The overpowering stench of human urine was rife as it ran down the open gullies through the market, intermingled with the bitter smell of raw dog meat, fresh snake's blood and gutted and plucked chickens that had been lying in the morning heat covered with flies still waiting to be purchased.

Right there, Kate resolved that if she ever bought a chicken in Vietnam, it would be a 'live one'—and she would deal with it herself.

With that thought, she focused on her original purpose. She needed to buy a selection of fruits and vegetables to use as props in her English class that evening. The Commander had informed her she'd be teaching on Wednesday, Thursday and Friday evenings during her first week.

Thankfully, Anne had helped her exchange US dollars into Vietnamese Dong (at roughly US $1 to 143 Vietnamese Dong) and advised her to barter fiercely. Everything would be at least four times the normal price for a white expat like her.

Kate took a deep breath and stepped back into the fray, determined to navigate the market with a little more confidence this time.

She felt entirely in her element as she bartered at the market. Despite the language barrier, she managed to fill her basket with a variety of items and still had plenty of change left over.

Later that day, Kate and Stuart moved into what was generously described as a 'hotel.' The room was cramped, dark and dismal. The bed was rock hard, and the linen carried a pungent smell of sewage. It was, to put it mildly, far from comfortable. A dusty television, which looked as though it hadn't been used since the 1970s, stood unsteadily atop a rickety table. A single lightbulb hung from the centre of the ceiling, though its utility was limited since electricity was only available for a couple of hours each day.

Hoping to rid the room of the dreadful smell, Kate opened the window. The noise from the street below immediately assaulted her senses—motorbikes, animals, clanging cyclo bikes, ringing cycle bells and shouting people created an overwhelming cacophony. Kate sighed as she realized that although it was only February, the air was extremely warmer than she had anticipated and, with its oppressive humidity, would only make the stench worse. Quickly, she shut the window and sank to the floor, her head in her hands.

'What have we done? What have I done?' she said aloud, her voice tinged with despair.

'It'll be fine. We won't be staying here long,' Stuart reassured her. 'You'll find somewhere and barter a good deal— I'm sure of it.'

But Kate wasn't convinced. To secure a proper home, they needed a trading license, a reliable local contact and a trustworthy translator who wouldn't skim off bribes from property owners. Although she'd only been in Hanoi a couple of days, she already knew she couldn't imagine living in the city. The relentless noise, the pervasive smell of raw sewage, and the constant risk of accidents, like seeing cyclists knocked over as a regular occurrence, were far from her vision of 'home.'

***

The next morning, Kate shivered as she stepped out. It was February, and Hanoi's winter chill was biting in such a contrast to the previous day. Foolishly, she had packed only lightweight summer clothes for herself and Stuart while their warmer clothing was still en route in a shipping container that wouldn't arrive for another five weeks. Ken had mentioned that this winter was unusually cold, with temperatures hovering around 13°C and unlikely to rise beyond 15°C in the coming weeks. Resolving to find some warmer clothing locally, Kate added it to her growing mental to-do list.

Meanwhile, she struggled to prepare an English lesson. How on earth was she going to teach when she couldn't understand them, and they couldn't understand her? The idea felt like a nightmare. After some thought, a plan began to form in her mind. She would enlist a young Vietnamese gentleman to stand at the front with her. He could name the fruits and vegetables in Vietnamese while she provided the English translation. He could even write the Vietnamese words on the blackboard while she wrote the English ones. It was a simple plan, but it seemed feasible.

Later, as she climbed the five flights of stairs to the classroom, Kate found the humid air repressive despite the cooler weather. She was startled to see the classroom packed with police officers of all ages, immaculately dressed in dark green uniforms, sitting silently, all eyes fixed on her.

'Wow,' Kate said aloud, unable to contain her surprise.

'Chào buổi tối,' she greeted them nervously, crossing her fingers behind her back for luck.

'Chào buổi tối,' they replied in perfect unison, their robotic precision both impressive and unnerving.

Kate gestured for a young officer to join her at the front. She pulled a bag of bean sprouts from her basket and held it up for the class.

'Bean sprouts,' she said clearly.

'Giá đỗ,' the young officer replied.

'Bean sprouts,' Kate repeated, encouraging the entire class to join in.

'Bean sprouts,' they chanted together, their voices perfectly synchronized.

Pleased, Kate clapped her hands and smiled at her 'pupils' as she had decided to think of them. Calling them pupils rather than policemen made the situation feel less intimidating and more manageable.

For the next two hours, the lesson continued in the same manner. Kate held up each item from her basket, teaching them its English name while they supplied the Vietnamese equivalent. At the end of the class, she offered the fruits and vegetables to the officers, but none came forward to take them.

As they filed out at 7:30 p.m., each officer bowed politely to Kate. She realized she had genuinely enjoyed the lesson and felt proud of what she had achieved.

Kate made a mental note to ask Anne if there was an orphanage in Hanoi where she could donate the leftover produce.

In the days that followed, Kate and Stuart survived on chicken and rice from a nearby market stall. The dish was passable, though overly salty, and the rice was sticky and gloopy. Kate stuck to drinking the cans of cola she had packed in her suitcase, unable to stomach the green tea, condensed milk-laden coffee, or the questionable water quality of the bottled water. She looked forward to having her own home, where she could boil water properly and cook fresh meals.

Wherever she went, Kate noticed she was followed by a Vietnamese policeman. He made no effort to be discreet, trailing behind her, standing outside places she visited, or watching her and Stuart from across the road. Even when they went out in the evenings, he followed. Deciding to befriend him, Kate began bringing him coffee or bánh mì each morning and evening. He always accepted these gestures but refused when she once offered him chicken and rice.

A few days later, Stuart found Kate collapsed on the hotel bedroom floor. She didn't respond to his voice or touch. Panicked, Stuart called Ken, and together they rushed her to the local hospital.

When Kate finally regained consciousness, she felt a wave of nausea and vomited into a bowl Stuart had thoughtfully placed on her lap.

'Where am I? What happened? And why do I have these tubes in me?' Kate asked weakly.

'You're in the local hospital,' Stuart explained. 'You collapsed in the hotel bedroom, and Ken helped me bring you here. You're on a drip because you're severely dehydrated and have a dangerously high level of salt in your system.'

Stuart went on to explain that the doctor had attributed her condition to MSG—monosodium glutamate—commonly used in Vietnamese cooking. 'It's much more concentrated than regular salt and can cause dehydration, migraines and, in extreme cases, unconsciousness,' he said calmly.

Kate felt a tear roll down her cheek. 'When can I—' she began, but Stuart interrupted.

'The nice Australian doctor said you need to rest and rehydrate for a few days. Once your migraine clears, you can get back to things.'

Just then, a nurse appeared by Kate's bedside.

'Would you like a cup of tea?' she asked warmly, fluffing Kate's pillow with a genuine smile.

'With proper milk and a proper teabag?' Kate asked hopefully, as though she were requesting the crown jewels.

The nurse laughed. 'Of course! I'll bring two cups,' she said, glancing at Stuart.

True to her word, the nurse returned a short while later with two steaming mugs of tea. The milk tasted slightly different from what they were used to, but it was proper milk, and the tea was made with a proper teabag. Kate sipped it gratefully, savouring the small comfort.

Shortly after having his cup of tea, Stuart left to thank Ken for his earlier help; Kate allowed herself a moment to enjoy the tea. For the first time in days, she felt a flicker of hope.

'Sorry, I'm being so rude. Thank you so much. I'm so thirsty, and this is the first proper cup of tea I've had since we arrived,' Kate said, smiling up at the woman.

'What's your name?' Kate asked.

'Sophie,' the woman replied.

'Thank you, Sophie—you're quite literally a lifesaver. Any chance of another cup of tea, please? And do you know when I can leave here and have this drip removed?'

'I finish my shift in about an hour, and your fluid bag should be empty by then,' Sophie said with a warm smile. 'How about coming home with me for the afternoon? That way, I can keep an eye on you to make sure you're not overdoing it. I'll even make you some cheese on toast.'

'Cheese on toast!' Kate squealed, her face lighting up with excitement.

An hour later, Sophie returned to remove the needle from Kate's arm and escorted her to meet Mr Houng, the driver assigned to Kate and Stuart. They had been told they weren't allowed to drive themselves in Hanoi—foreigners were frequently stopped by police, often for arbitrary reasons, as a display of control or to extract bribes. They had also discovered that there were only about a dozen cars in the entire city at the time of their arrival.

As Mr Houng navigated the chaotic dirt roads, filled with potholes and teeming with cyclists, Kate marvelled at the sheer madness around her. Many of the cyclists carried livestock, multiple passengers, or impossibly large loads, weaving unpredictably through the traffic. There seemed to be no rules governing which side of the road to use or whether to stop at junctions—it was every man for himself. To make matters worse, Kate noticed that Mr Houng didn't turn on the car's headlights as dusk fell.

'Why don't you put the lights on?' she asked.

But despite her attempts to explain their importance, language barriers aside, Mr Houng wouldn't budge. Apparently, many Vietnamese drivers believed that keeping the lights off conserved fuel.

After about ten minutes, they arrived at Sophie's home on the outskirts of Nghi Tam, also known as the Flower Village. As Kate stepped out of the car, she was struck by the clean, fresh air and the relative quiet of the area.

'Come in,' Sophie said lovingly.

Kate entered and immediately felt at ease. The house was comfortable and inviting, with a homely charm that stood in stark contrast to the harshness of Hanoi. Kate felt truly relaxed as she walked into Sophie's home.

Over lunch, Sophie shared her story. Originally from Wales, she had travelled to Australia in her early twenties, where, within the first two weeks of her arrival, she met the man who would become her husband. They married and spent the years that followed living and working around the world due to her husband's career managing large corporate building projects.

The couple had arrived in Hanoi four months earlier than Kate and Stuart, with their two young children—Freddie, aged four, and Florence, who was just two. Kate admired Sophie's positive outlook, especially given the challenges of raising small children in such a foreign environment.

Sophie explained that she worked part-time at the local Bupa clinic, which wasn't a full hospital but was well-equipped by Hanoi standards. The clinic also maintained a consulting room within the main local hospital to ensure expatriates received the best care possible and had a translator on hand. Kate recalled her own brief experience there—it had felt chaotic and lacking in resources, but she'd been unconscious on arrival, and from what Stuart had said, there wasn't any choice at the time, so she decided not to judge too harshly.

Sophie told her about the children's schooling. Florence attended a nearby crèche, conveniently located next to the Bupa clinic, while Freddie was enrolled in an expatriate school with mostly South Korean children attending at the time. Sophie expressed her hope that the promised Hanoi International School would open soon. The school was planned as a joint venture between the Centre for Education

Technology and International School Development Inc. It would offer the International Baccalaureate (IB) curriculum and provide a truly international learning environment.

During the 1990s, international education in Hanoi was still in its infancy. The United Nations International School (UNIS), which opened in 1988 with just four students, was one of the only options. It had since expanded rapidly, catering to students from pre-kindergarten to grade 12 and following the IB programme to prepare them for further education abroad. Morning Star International School, another option, was a partnership with Texas Christian School, offering education to children from four months old to grade 12. Both schools focused on fostering multicultural communities, with students from countries including Vietnam, Japan, Germany, the UK, the US and Australia.

'It's a fantastic opportunity for Freddie and Florence to learn different languages and cultures from such a young age,' Sophie said. 'It'll only enhance their education. It is incredible how quickly young children pick up new languages. I marvel when I watch them playing together as they interact in Japanese, Korean, French, German and English.'

By the time Kate realised how late it was, darkness had fallen. She felt she had overstayed her welcome and reluctantly prepared to leave.

'Thank you so much for your kind hospitality and for making me feel so welcome, Sophie,' Kate said as she stepped outside to meet Mr Houng.

'It's been lovely, and it was no trouble at all,' Sophie replied warmly. She handed Kate a slip of paper. 'Here's my number. If you need anything—or just fancy catching up over a cuppa—give me a call.'

Kate smiled as she tucked the number safely into her bag. 'Just one thing, Sophie, is there any reason why you chose to live on the outskirts of Nghi Tam rather than in the flower village itself?'

Laughing, Sophie replied, 'Because, with two small children, I didn't fancy having to walk a distance to our home, especially during the wet seasons. All the mud and mess that goes with it.'

Kate felt awful knowing that Mr Houng had sat outside in his car all afternoon, refusing to take a break or go home until she was ready to be taken back to the hotel. Sophie had even enlisted her Vietnamese friend to translate a few times, but Mr Houng remained steadfast, insisting he would wait.

When he finally dropped Kate off at the hotel, she gave him a grateful wave and watched as he drove away. Back in the dimly lit and dingy room, she collapsed onto the hard bed, where Stuart hugged her close. Exhausted, she closed her eyes and quickly drifted off to sleep.

Chapter 8: Roots in the Flower Village

Several hours later, Kate awoke from a vivid dream about food. In her mind's eye, she had seen a pork joint roasting to perfection. The pale cream rind slowly transformed into golden crackling, glistening as bubbles formed and burst on its surface. She could almost hear the crackling hiss and pop in the oven tray, its juices sizzling as steam rose to fill the air with the sweet, savoury aroma of roasting pork. In the dream, she had removed the crackling and left the joint to rest, seasoning it carefully before covering it again. The crackling, placed on kitchen roll to absorb excess fat, was returned to the oven to keep warm. She could almost taste the succulent meat as her teeth sank into it, each bite rich, tender and satisfying.

When Kate woke fully, her mouth was watering, and her nostrils flared in anticipation of smells that weren't there. Hunger gnawed at her stomach. She reached for a bánh mì and bit into it, though it didn't come close to the meal from her dream.

As she chewed, doubts began creeping back into her mind. She questioned her decision to uproot their lives, dragging Stuart and herself away from the comfort and security they had enjoyed back home. Picking up her Filofax, she turned to the front page, where she had written a motivational reminder that she had seen in a book some years back; she referred to it often:

The worst beliefs you can have are 'self-limiting beliefs.' For example, you may think yourself to be less talented or capable than others. You may think that others are superior to you in some way. You may have fallen into the common trap of selling yourself short and settling for far less than you are truly capable of. These self-limiting beliefs act like brakes on your potential. They hold you back. They generate the two greatest enemies of personal success. Doubt and fear. They paralyse you and cause you to hesitate to take the intelligent risks that are necessary to fulfil your true potential. For you to progress, to move onward and upward in your life and your business, you must continually challenge your self-limiting beliefs. You must reject any thought or suggestion that you are limited in any way. You must accept as a basic principle that you are a 'no-limit' person, and that what others have done is also possible for you to achieve.

Brian Tracy

'I'm going to write this out on a large piece of paper and stick it on the wall in our home and office. That way, when we're feeling low, we'll see it and remind ourselves to carry on and not give in. *It's similar to what my Nan used to tell me to do. 'Write down your dreams, Kate. Nothing is impossible just believe in your dreams,'* Kate said to Stuart.

'Vietnam is definitely a country where you either sink or swim. There's no room to drift here,' Kate said with a sigh.

The next morning, Stuart left for Bangkok for five days to sort out the operational paperwork required for their joint venture. He also planned to spend time with the team there, learning more about customs and shipping processes across Asia Pacific, Europe and the US.

Kate, meanwhile, was determined to find a house as soon as possible. She knew it was critical to create a proper home—a space where they could enjoy privacy, relax and welcome family or friends who might visit. She had set her heart on living in Nghi Tam, the Flower Village, a historic area known for its beauty and charm.

For centuries, Nghi Tam had been one of the largest flower villages in the region, supplying fresh blooms to Hanoi and its surroundings. Nearly all households in the 1950s had been involved in cultivating flowers. The village was graced by landmarks like Kim Lien Pagoda and the Nghi Tam Communal House, which embodied the area's cultural richness. The glistening lake, abundant wildlife and vibrant flower gardens created a picturesque setting, though Kate knew the peace would be punctuated by the sounds of livestock and the frequent tannoy announcements from the government.

Kate accompanied Stuart to the airport, partly for the experience and partly to see if the Mekong River, which had been alarmingly high on their arrival, had receded. The dirt tracks were chaotic as ever, with Mr Houng weaving carefully through the sea of pushbikes. Dust rose in thick clouds, obscuring the road ahead like a foggy blanket.

The airport was just as frenetic as it had been on their first day.

'Good luck, and enjoy!' Kate said as Stuart headed to the Vietnam Airlines check-in desk.

'Oh, and don't forget to look for hot water bottles if you get time!' she called after him, smiling.

After dropping Stuart off, Mr Houng drove Kate to the entrance of Nghi Tam village. Cars could not drive around the village as there were no roads, just narrow footpaths. She met a local woman named Phuong, who showed her around nine properties.

Four were incomplete building sites, and another four were cramped, insecure and poorly built. The ninth house, however, stood out. It had a spacious, established garden surrounded by a fence, four bedrooms, two bathrooms and a large empty room designated as the kitchen next to another large room that could be used as their lounge and dining room. Balconies extended from each bedroom, with two offering stunning views of the lake. Inside, the marble floors and grand staircase lent a sense of elegance.

Of course, there were challenges. The house lacked central heating, which wasn't uncommon in Vietnam, but Kate remembered packing three small electric radiators in their shipment. The windows would need curtains, and she'd have to figure out how to connect the gas cooker and washing machine—despite the apparent absence of plumbing in the kitchen. But Kate reassured herself, 'It's all part of the adventure.'

She inspected the finer details, testing the toilets, showers and lights. Ideally, she would have liked to see how the house held up in the rain, but the sunny, dry day offered no such opportunity.

'Phoung, tell the agent we'll negotiate a monthly rent,' Kate said, trying not to show her excitement.

Nearly three hours later, a rent was agreed upon, and the terms finalised. Kate's only lingering concern was the mosquitos. In the Flower Village, near the lake, they would possibly be a constant nuisance. She was already enduring about 20 bites a day, her legs itchy and swollen despite applying an Australian repellent called *Rid*. The cream smelled dreadful but worked well enough to stop bites from blistering.

As she stood outside the house, gazing at the shimmering lake, Kate felt a sense of accomplishment. It wasn't perfect, but it was theirs—and it was the start of building a 'home.'

Kate returned to the hotel smiling, her mind already whirring as she began drafting yet another 'to-do' list. She decided to pop over to the office, which was open, to spend some time with the two women working there. These women had been recruited by a remarkable Filipino gentleman who had come to Hanoi ahead of Stuart and herself to find an office and establish the operational structure. He had already built solid connections at the port and with customs officials to handle imports and the Embassies in Hanoi, but the head office wanted more. The joint venture partnership signed in Bangkok aimed to generate direct business development and secure larger volumes of moves into all areas of Vietnam and across other countries within the region.

Kate knew her immediate focus had to be on cultivating relationships with major international corporations, especially those expanding from their home countries. She also planned to connect with her company's global offices to identify businesses setting up operations in Vietnam, Cambodia and Laos. Partnering with relocation and removal agents in many countries would be crucial to securing at least the import of clients' containers and air freight, if not the entire shipment process from packing to delivery. It was a monumental task.

While cleaning the office, Kate struck up a conversation with the two women. She explained that she was teaching English to the local police and army three evenings a week and asked if they might like to join her classes.

Houng, a tall and striking woman, exuded a sense of strength and survival, though Kate detected a sly cunning beneath her composed exterior. She estimated Houng to be in her late twenties and noted that she was the more outspoken of the two.

Hun, in contrast, was petite, with a warm, welcoming smile. She had a naturally helpful nature, always eager to assist Kate with whatever she was doing. Hun seemed to speak from the heart, making her openness to change a sharp contrast to Houng's more guarded demeanour.

Both women were dressed in the traditional *áo dài,* an elegant outfit that Kate found captivating. The ensemble consisted of silk trousers paired with a long silk tunic, typically embroidered, with long sleeves and slits at the sides to allow for ease of movement. While white and brown were common colours, Kate admired the vibrant hues often chosen for special occasions. She learned that colour in Vietnam held symbolic meaning: red signified good luck and prosperity, often worn during *Tết* (Lunar New Year) or weddings; white symbolised purity and was worn by young schoolgirls. Women also selected colours based on the elements associated with their birth years—metal, wood, water, fire, or earth.

Kate made a mental note: 'Stop asking so many questions at once!' She was naturally inquisitive and prone to bombarding people with her endless 'whys.' Returning to the moment, she focused on the conversation.

Houng and Hun communicated, with some difficulty, that it would be impossible for women to attend her English classes. Kate was taken aback.

This was like a red rag to a bull for Kate. *It's 1994!* she thought. *Women should have equal rights and access to education, regardless of the country or its political system.* Determined, she resolved to open her classes to women and men of all ages and professions, not just male police officers, army and government officials.

That evening, Kate brought a translated note to her class. It requested a larger room, more chalk, and permission to open the classes to local people—men and women alike—free of charge. If the Vietnamese government truly wanted English to become their second language, she reasoned, they needed to provide opportunities for everyone to learn.

The room erupted into commotion after Kate handed over the note. Raised voices and heated discussions followed, and soon, the Commander entered, gesturing for Kate to leave the classroom.

Kate's heart raced as he shouted at her, joined by another man in uniform. Tears began streaming down her cheeks. She panicked, convinced she was about to be arrested for speaking out.

Then Ken rushed through the door.

'I'm so sorry, Ken. Why have they called you here?' Kate asked, her voice trembling.

'Well,' Ken replied with a sigh, 'you've spoken out, and in Vietnam, that's not seen as acceptable—especially for a woman.'

'I only suggested opening the class to more people, including women,' Kate said defensively. 'What are they saying?'

'They're arguing about whether to allow other men in, let alone women,' Ken explained.

Kate's shoulders slumped. 'Oh God, I'm going to be thrown in prison, aren't I?'

Ken smiled reassuringly. 'Not quite. Just wait.'

After a tense pause, the Commander turned to Kate. 'You teach English to any man or woman?' he asked.

'Yes, please,' Kate said quickly, with Ken translating.

'We decide soon,' the Commander said before leaving the room.

'Thank you so much,' Kate replied, tears still in her eyes.

As the commotion subsided, Kate turned to Ken. 'I'm truly sorry for dragging you into this. I shouldn't have made this your problem.'

'Don't worry, Kate,' Ken said with a grin. 'I think they might allow it. If they do, it'll be worth celebrating—big time. Whoop whoop! This will make for an interesting Hash name.'

Kate returned to her lesson, using a different student to translate her words. She held up items and objects, saying the English word, and they translated into Vietnamese while she wrote them on the board. The class repeated the English words in unison, sounding more like a regiment on parade. That evening's theme was household items, as Kate had found it easy to source props like baskets, sweeping brushes, bins and chopsticks. She had borrowed most of these items from the 'hotel' and Hun.

To her surprise, Kate noticed that her students were becoming more receptive. A few even smiled during the lesson, a rare sight. Slowly but surely, they seemed to be warming to her, and she felt a growing sense of accomplishment.

Chapter 9: Silk, Sweat and Beer

The following day, Kate attended a reception hosted by the Canadian Embassy, meeting representatives from most of the Embassies based in Hanoi. She was pleasantly surprised by how down-to-earth the Ambassadors were. In her experience back in London, Embassy representatives had carried an air of statesmanship, almost a hierarchical aloofness. Here, however, they were approachable, engaging and refreshingly normal—simply people doing a job for their country and its citizens in the region.

The Canadian ambassador, one of the few women in such a position in Vietnam at the time, particularly stood out to Kate. It struck her that this was a new era, with Western society beginning to demonstrate to Vietnamese women that anything was possible if they believed in themselves. This realisation strengthened Kate's resolve to push for access to her English classes for Vietnamese women. During her various conversations, Kate explained to people what she had been asked to do by the Commander and that she was aiming to open the classes up to as many local Vietnamese men and women as possible.

Later that afternoon, Kate attended another group meeting, this time exclusively for women. The gathering included the wives of ambassadors, civil servants (a term Kate found outdated and cold) and a handful of expatriate wives whose husbands were stationed in Vietnam. Many of these women had opted to live in Hanoi for its relative tranquillity and safety compared to the bustling chaos of Ho Chi Minh City (HCMC), where their husbands primarily worked.

Kate had three goals in attending the meeting. Firstly, she sought to establish connections with embassies to secure future relocation contracts, ensuring both outgoing and incoming staff moves were handled seamlessly. Secondly, she hoped these women might support her efforts to fundraise and volunteer to support Vietnamese orphans. She had been deeply disturbed by the sight of so many young, vulnerable and displaced children, and she was determined to improve their living conditions. Just as importantly, Kate wanted to hopefully meet some like-minded women and develop friendships – even if it was just a couple of women she could eventually call 'friends.'

Kate mentally added another item to her ever-growing to-do list: find a suitable building for a home for these children. Though she thrived on challenges and working under pressure, she wondered if she was setting herself an unrealistic goal, given she had only been in Hanoi for just over two months.

From the outset, Kate and Stuart had agreed to maintain boundaries in their work to ensure the business ran smoothly and their relationship remained intact. Stuart focused on operations, while Kate handled business development. They recognized there would inevitably be some overlap, but defining their roles helped avoid unnecessary tension.

They also agreed on the importance of regularly visiting HCMC to establish themselves there. Stuart, in particular, emphasized the need to focus on business development rather than operations, given that the operational team in HCMC was already managed from Bangkok.

That evening, they attended a dinner hosted by the incoming New Zealand Ambassador, whose shipment was due to arrive the following month. Although the dinner was described as informal, Kate felt underdressed. Most of her evening wear was still in the container, so she had to make do with what she had.

The evening, however, turned out to be delightful. The New Zealand Embassy staff gave Kate and Stuart a warm and genuine welcome. Kate was pleased to see Sophie and her husband there, along with Ken, Anne and several women from the embassy lunch.

As they returned to their hotel that night, Kate reflected that the event had been thoroughly enjoyable.

The next day, Hun agreed to take Kate to a local dressmaker after Kate had secured Stuart's permission to 'borrow' her for the morning. Kate had never been particularly interested in fashion and owned only a modest wardrobe, so the prospect of bespoke tailoring felt both novel and daunting.

Following Hun through a narrow doorway that barely clung to its hinges, Kate found herself in a dimly lit room, illuminated only by a lantern and a few flickering candles. The electricity had been off since early that morning—the fourth outage that week.

Four women entered through a curtain at the back of the room. The three younger women giggled nervously while the fourth—a hunched, frail figure with skin like weathered leather—regarded Kate with a stern expression. The older woman, who Kate assumed was Mrs Wang, took Kate's hands in her own. Her long, crooked fingers were surprisingly soft as she gently traced Kate's fingers and turned her palms upward for inspection.

'Mrs. Wang, this is Miss Kate. She would like dresses and other clothes,' Hun explained in Vietnamese.

Mrs. Wang cupped Kate's face with her hands, holding it for a brief moment before sliding her hands down Kate's neck, shoulders, and arms. Kate froze, as Mrs. Wang continued her measurements by running her hands down Kate's sides, waist and legs—finishing with a sweep over her stomach and breasts.

'It's OK, Miss Kate. She is measuring you,' Hun said in her broken English.

'But she isn't using a tape measure,' Kate replied, startled.

Hun looked puzzled. Kate would later learn that tape measures were virtually unheard of in Hanoi.

As Mrs. Wang worked, the younger women held various fabrics against Kate's face, gauging which colours suited her best. Kate decided on four shift dresses—simple and cool, suitable for both informal evenings and formal daytime meetings. Each would be paired with a short, tailored jacket.

One fabric, a navy cashmere and silk blend, stood out. It was luxuriously soft, and Kate decided to have a long-sleeved jacket, skirt, trousers, and short-sleeved dress made from it. For the shift dresses, she selected vibrant raw silks: one in bright red, another in lime green, a striking orange and a classic black. Unable to resist, she also chose a beautiful purple linen/silk mixed fabric for a pair of trousers and a matching jacket.

As the list of garments grew, Kate felt a pang of guilt. The extravagance seemed at odds with the suffering she had witnessed among Hanoi's orphans.

'Hun, I can't do this. It feels disrespectful to the children and to you. And besides, it must be so expensive—Stuart will be furious,' Kate said, forgetting that Hun likely didn't understand.

Moments later, Hun handed Kate a piece of paper with the total cost: $120.

'What? Oh my God, no way! Are you sure this is the correct price, Hun? For everything?' Kate exclaimed.

Mrs. Wang and Hun simply shrugged, their expressions calm and matter-of-fact.

Kate stared at the number in disbelief. For the first time that day, she felt truly indulgent—but also oddly reassured.

Four days later, Kate's order of clothes was delivered to the office. Excitedly, she carried them back to the hotel to try them on. Each item fitted perfectly, showcasing immaculate craftsmanship. The fabrics were fully lined, beautifully tailored, and looked stunning. Kate was delighted, and to her surprise, she actually enjoyed the experience of trying them on. The silk felt cool, smooth, and soft against her skin, its texture almost alive. It was both practical and luxurious—a strong natural material that symbolised resilience as much as elegance.

To express her gratitude, Kate gave Hun a bouquet of flowers, carefully timing the gesture for when Houng was out of the office to avoid any appearance of favouritism. Hun was clearly touched, and Kate felt a warm glow of satisfaction.

To her surprise, Stuart was thrilled by her experience at the dressmaker's. She had suggested he might like to go along himself someday, but he dismissed the idea with a chuckle and a shake of his head.

Kate, meanwhile, was busy drafting a newsletter for distribution to her UK head office, top international clients, global agents, and international companies operating in Vietnam. The aim was to increase awareness of their services and reinforce their readiness to assist with relocations across Vietnam. She began jotting down content ideas for the newsletter:

Do Ladies Perspire, Sweat or Glow? Reflecting on the necessity of changing clothes three or four times a day in 100% humidity and temperatures of 35–38°C. How long does it take to acclimatize to such conditions?

What Not to Pack for Vietnam: Books, magazines, photo albums, records, cassettes and maps—and why they don't fare well in the humid climate.

The Mystery of MSG: What it is, its implications for health, and how to request food without it.

Packing Tips: Essential items to include in your shipping container when relocating to Vietnam.

That Saturday, Ken invited Kate and Stuart to join in on the 'Hash.'

The Hash House Harriers, as Ken explained, was an international social running club. Events, known as 'Hashes,' were non-competitive runs held weekly. Typically, a small team of 'Hares' scouted a 5-kilometre route earlier in the week, often through rice fields, forests, remote roads or buffalo-filled fields. On Saturday morning, the Hares would mark the trail with flour, including false trails, to add an element of challenge. Participants then met at a designated starting point to follow the true trail while avoiding the decoys.

Ken warned Kate and Stuart to be prepared for mud, water and general messiness—and a round of forfeits and games, usually involving drinking, at the end. The tradition dates back to the 1940s, though Ken wasn't entirely sure whether it originated in Malaysia or Brighton.

Kate and Stuart had made a pact to finish work by noon on Saturdays to give themselves and their staff in the office and warehouse a proper break. They knew the workload would only increase in the months ahead, and they were determined to set boundaries to avoid burnout.

That afternoon, Mr Houng waited for them outside the office. His car, an old but impeccably maintained model that might have been a Ford Cortina, gleamed as always. Mr Houng took great pride in his role as their driver, and Kate respected his dedication. Married with two young children, he was about Stuart's age, though they mainly communicated through hand gestures and pointing to her watch.

Kate had insisted that Mr Houng could go home while they attended evening events, but he always stayed until the dinner or gathering was over. She admired his work ethic and respected his decision.

Before they left for the Hash, another Embassy driver had advised Mr Houng to line the car's back seats and floors with cardboard. Heeding this advice, he meticulously prepared the car to protect it from mud. Kate couldn't fault his reasoning— she would have done the same.

Armed with a chicken *bánh mì* and a change of clothes packed in the car, Kate and Stuart set off. The journey was a bumpy one, with Mr Houng skillfully navigating dirt tracks crowded with cyclists, horse-drawn carts, tuk-tuks, wandering buffalo, and the occasional rickety old lorry speeding dangerously close. The dust was so thick it felt like driving through a sandstorm. Kate made a mental note to bring a cushion for future trips, as every jolt from the car's worn suspension left her aching.

When they arrived, Kate stepped out of the car and immediately noticed the fresher air. Though it was hot and humid, the atmosphere felt cleaner and less oppressive.

Her attention was drawn to a man in the river across the track, guiding a narrow bamboo boat across the water. In front of the boat, four buffalo waded, their movements slow and deliberate. The boat was crudely constructed from bamboo canes bound together with vines. On the opposite bank, a woman dressed in a traditional *áo dài* and conical hat waited patiently. Nearby, hessian sacks lay scattered on the ground, and a bamboo hut perched on stilts that looked like large trees that had been cut down, offering a raised platform seemingly built with the same vine bindings. The river sparkled in the sunlight, its fast-moving current clear and inviting.

It was a scene of simplicity, ingenuity, and beauty. Kate felt compelled to capture the moment.

She rushed back to the car for her camera, a cheap but reliable device she carried everywhere. Since arriving in Hanoi, Kate had taken hundreds of photos. Stuart often teased her about her obsession, but Kate didn't care.

'Making memories for when we're old and past it,' she had told him the first time he questioned her enthusiasm.

Around twenty people gathered at the Hash meeting point, a welcoming mix of nationalities—mostly embassy staff with a few local Vietnamese participants. Kate quickly noted, with some relief, that almost everyone was dressed in old, well-worn trainers, scruffy T-shirts, and shorts. There was no sign of the latest sportswear trends here.

Note to self: keep a couple of pairs of trainers, shorts, and at least a dozen old T-shirts specifically for Hashing, Kate thought, filing it away as a mental reminder.

Kate and Stuart were formally introduced to the group, though she doubted she'd remember all their names. The basic rules of the run were explained, and soon they were off. The group set out at a gentle jog along a dirt track that ran beside the river. Kate stuck with the main group, feeling safer in numbers for her first experience of the Hash, even as a few more adventurous participants darted off to explore alternate trails.

The route followed the river, offering captivating glimpses of rural life. Kate watched as women paddled small bamboo boats across the water with practised ease. To her amazement, she spotted three men riding buffalo through the river, their animals moving steadily against the current.

Her camera was practically glued to her eye as she snapped away, capturing every moment. She was fascinated by the women's attire—black trousers paired with long-sleeved tops, with the older women wearing brown tops. What struck her most was that the fabric seemed to be predominantly silk. Back home, silk was a luxury reserved for special occasions, but here, it was a practical everyday material, likely chosen for its breathable fibres, durability, and ability to keep the wearer cool in the humid climate.

Each woman wore a conical hat, a staple she had noticed across all age groups since arriving in Hanoi. These hats, Kate thought, were not only protection from the sun but also practical shields against rain and mosquitos.

'Get back with the group and stop hiding behind the lens,' Kate muttered to herself, reluctantly lowering the camera.

After roughly 2.5 kilometres, the route turned away from the river and into the paddy fields. The lush green expanse stretched as far as the eye could see, and despite the mud, Kate couldn't resist pulling her camera out again. The sweetcorn plantations on the one side towered above the paddy fields on the other. Chuckling to herself, she realised she was falling into her usual habit of getting lost in her own little world. Stuart was up ahead with the main group, leaving her to bring up the rear.

Each step through the paddy fields was a challenge. The mud oozed around her trainers, squelching audibly as it seeped between her toes and clung to her calves. The deeper the mud got, the harder it became to lift her feet, the suction pulling at her with every step. It was exhausting work, but Kate was determined to keep going. She silently thanked her luck for not falling over—or worse, dropping her camera.

How on earth am I going to get all this film developed? Kate wondered. She had already used 14 rolls of 36 exposures each since arriving in Vietnam and had packed plenty more for the trip. Still, she hadn't yet figured out where to process them or how to restock her supply.

Eventually, the group returned to the starting point. Everyone gathered in a circle, and Kate and Stuart were called into the middle as newcomers. They were officially introduced to the Hanoi Hash House Harriers, but their initiation came with a twist: forfeits.

Stuart went first, handed a raw, plucked and gutted chicken filled with beer. He was instructed to drink the beer from inside the bird. He looked at Kate with a mix of horror and disbelief, but she nodded her encouragement despite clutching her own stomach in silent dread. Somehow, Stuart managed to do it without a grimace, earning cheers from the crowd.

Then, it was Kate's turn.

The chicken felt unpleasantly warm in her hands, and the smell was overwhelming. Her stomach churned as panic set in. *Salmonella, or worse,* she thought. The group began chanting, 'Down! Down! Down!' as she brought the chicken closer to her lips.

Resolving not to touch the bird's beak, Kate held it by the breast, tilted it carefully and allowed a trickle of beer to reach her mouth. She immediately spat it out, gagging as the sour taste hit her.

How did Stuart manage this without flinching? she wondered, suppressing the urge to retch.

Next, they were each handed a bottle of *33 Beer,* a popular Vietnamese brew, and instructed to down it in one go. Kate managed it without hesitation, reasoning that the beer might help sterilize her mouth and stomach while washing away the foul taste of the chicken. Her only concern was whether the rumours about Vietnamese beer containing formaldehyde were true.

The group erupted into thunderous applause as Kate and Stuart completed their initiation. They were officially welcomed into the Hash House Harriers with cheers and good-natured laughter.

Returning to the car, Mr Houng beamed with a broad smile, clapping his hands enthusiastically. Kate couldn't fathom why he seemed so pleased. She and Stuart were drenched, covered in a messy combination of mud and beer from their escapades. Changing clothes wasn't an option, but both were deeply grateful for the cardboard Mr Houng had thoughtfully placed on the back seats and floor to protect the car's interior.

'We really ought to start keeping towels in the car for these Hashes,' Kate remarked, her tone slightly apologetic. 'It's not fair on Mr Houng to have to sit in the car with us while we're soaking wet and reeking.'

As Kate wiped the sweat and mud from her brow, she reflected on the experience. Despite the challenges—both physical and gastronomic—it had been an unforgettable day one she was certain would make its way into her growing collection of vivid memories from Vietnam.

Chapter 10: In the Heart of Hanoi

That Sunday, Kate and Stuart had spent hours wandering the streets, looking for items to furnish their new home. The city's labyrinthine streets each seemed to specialise in a particular trade. One road was devoted entirely to mechanics, lined with shops selling vehicle parts—motorbikes, scooters and everything in between. Most of the items looked like relics from the 1970s or probably earlier, Kate mused; their wear and tear was evidence of years of use.

Another street dazzled with the vibrant colours of silk, where tiny outlets displayed endless rolls of shimmering fabric in every hue imaginable. Yet another was crammed with household products: delicate tea sets, tiny rice bowls, chopsticks and small sweeping brushes crafted with elaborate detail. As they meandered through the streets, Kate diligently jotted down notes about what each area offered, envisioning future trips to pick up the perfect items.

Their explorations led them into the enchanting maze of 'The Old Quarters,' a place Kate immediately fell in love with. 'I can see myself spending hours here with my camera,' she told Stuart. The area radiated a magical, almost mysterious atmosphere, its appeal heightened by the faded facades and the robust activity that felt timeless. Children played in the narrow streets, and the elders crouched down, playing what Kate thought might be similar to drafts. Intrigued, she'd have to find out the name of the game. Food vendors were busy, and the aromas lingered in the air. There was a beautiful café full of people. The noise coming from it was intoxicating – she wanted to go in, but time was sadly against them.

Monday brought momentous news.

Kate and Stuart were finally handed the keys to what would soon become their home in Nghi Tam Village. To add to their excitement, they learned that their shipping container had arrived at the port and was awaiting customs clearance. Kate's heart raced with anticipation.

Ken, ever the helpful colleague, had offered to accompany Stuart to the port for the initial visit. Since it was a British shipment for a British client, he assured them his presence could smooth things over. 'You'll need to pay the "tea money",' Ken reminded them wryly, 'to ensure the container clears customs efficiently.'

Later that day, Stuart rang Ken to finalise their plan to visit the port.

'Hope you like whisky,' Ken quipped just before hanging up.

Stuart groaned inwardly. He couldn't stand spirits, whisky least of all, save for the occasional splash in an Irish coffee. He smiled at the memory of Kate's culinary flair. Her Irish coffees were legendary, as were the continental warm drinks and cocktails she whipped up for their famous parties. Their cocktail gatherings had always been a highlight, with friends raving about her creations.

While Stuart and Ken prepared for their port visit, Kate had a packed morning of appointments with various embassies. Her goal was to discuss their relocation requirements for the coming year. She planned to draft a calendar of anticipated moves, aligning embassy rotations with the influx of corporate relocations she'd started securing.

In the UK, Kate had honed her skill in spotting business opportunities by scouring newspapers for mergers, acquisitions and major appointments. These leads had often translated into contracts for relocating key personnel. Now, she faced a new challenge: 'How am I going to get this kind of information here?' she muttered to herself.

Later in the afternoon, Kate planned to visit their new home. She needed to measure for curtains and assess what else required attention before moving in. She also intended to visit the furniture warehouse, though calling it a 'warehouse' felt generous. In reality, it was a sprawling, ramshackle structure crammed with discarded furniture from various embassies. Kate had long resolved to inventory the items and propose selling them on behalf of their owners. 'It would save taxpayer money and free up space,' she reasoned, already anticipating the logistical challenges of moving everything to a proper warehouse in the future. It was another reason to get rid of all of the said items.

The ever-diligent Hun had arranged for a motorcycle taxi to take her to the house.

'Are you sure, Miss Kate? Dangerous on roads. You sit on the side of bike?' Hun asked with a furrowed brow.

Kate smiled reassuringly. 'Thank you, Hun, but I'll be fine. Please ask the driver to wait for me at the house and bring me back to the office when I'm ready. Side saddle, you mean?' she asked, now curious.

'Yes, Miss Kate. Safer for you.'

The motorcycle was an ancient relic. Kate, who was no expert on bikes, thought it looked like something from the 1950s. The driver, a wiry man with an ageing face, greeted her with a toothy smile. She noticed his long, dirt-caked fingernails, a common sight among men in Hanoi. Why did they keep their nails so long? It was yet another cultural mystery she added to her mental list of things to research.

'Hold onto his waist, Miss Kate, so you don't fall,' Hun instructed.

The ride was anything but comfortable. Sitting on 'side saddle' felt precarious, and the bumpy, rain-soaked roads did little to ease her nerves. The seat beneath her felt like it had spikes poking through the fabric. By the time they reached the narrow dirt path leading into Nghi Tam Village, Kate's legs were splattered with mud, and her patience was wearing thin.

The village entrance was marked by an ornate, carved arch adorned with detailed engravings of animals. To her right, a six-foot fence enclosed a construction site, its gaps revealing cranes and piles of building materials. A small bamboo-and-mud hut stood just beyond, supplementing the rustic surroundings.

Despite the discomfort of the journey, Kate couldn't help but marvel at the charm of her new neighbourhood.

Inside the small hut sat a woman who, to Kate's eyes, might have been in her early thirties—though that was purely a guess. Her face turned upwards with a broad smile, revealing teeth stained bright red, likely from betel nut chewing. Somehow, the cigarette perched unsteadily between her teeth remained in place, perhaps wedged into a gap. The woman's sun-ravaged skin bore deep lines, each seeming to tell a story of hardship and resilience. She gestured towards her motorbike parked beside the hut, its faded paintwork hinting at years of service.

Kate, without thinking, dismounted the bike and promptly landed in a puddle, her feet sinking into the muddy water. Already damp, her shoes were now completely soaked. Frustration flared momentarily, but she quickly brushed it aside and made her way over to greet the woman.

'Hello,' Kate said warmly, extending her hand. The woman responded with a firm and meaningful handshake. Her palm felt rough and boney. 'Message to self – speak Vietnamese!' Kate shouted to herself.

As Kate glanced inside the hut, she noticed a hand protruding through a small hole in the wall. The woman casually handed over a Western cigarette and accepted a crumpled Vietnamese Dong note in return. Peering further, Kate saw shelves stocked with cigarettes and local food items. It became clear this was a makeshift shop, cleverly positioned to serve the workers on the construction site behind the fence.

'How entrepreneurial,' Kate thought, smiling to herself. This simple yet ingenious setup intrigued her and sparked an idea. She decided to write a letter, have it translated and offer the woman a job as her daily driver. This would free up Mr Houng for Stuart to meet clients and conduct their surveys, which would become more frequent as the business grew. Moreover, travelling with the woman would give Kate an opportunity to learn more about Hanoi's culture and language.

Excited by the thought, Kate pulled out her phone and rang Stuart.

'Hi! How's it going? Are you still at the port? Did you manage to get the container cleared? When do we get our "home?' she rattled off in one breath.

'Slow down, Kate,' Stuart said, laughing. 'Yes, it's cleared. Ken managed to negotiate the "tea money," and the container's being delivered to the warehouse today.'

'That's amazing! You're both fantastic!' Kate replied enthusiastically. 'Any chance we can get it delivered to the house tomorrow? Please?' she added, using her most persuasive tone.

'I'll do my best to arrange it,' Stuart said. 'I'll need to find a tuk-tuk and a van—maybe Mr Houng can help. Oh, by the way, customs officials went through our photo albums and books.'

'What? Why?' Kate asked, horrified. Then she remembered what she'd learned in her first week—no Western influences, including books, photographs or newspapers, were allowed. It was deemed propaganda and a threat to the communist state's ideology.

'Any chance you can get them to return our books, etc., on the basis that I need them to teach English to the police and army officials?' Kate asked Stuart with a glimmer of hope in her voice.

Stuart explained the situation to Ken regarding the books and photo albums and asked if he could speak to the police commander to retrieve them so that Kate could use them for the English lessons. Ken laughed. 'She doesn't want much, does she? I'll see what I can do.'

'Thanks, Ken. In Kate's eyes, you will be an even bigger star,' Stuart said, relieved.

As Kate made her way to the house, butterflies danced in her stomach. Opening the gate, she was greeted by the lush fragrance of plants and flowers, their scents mingling in the humid air. The garden felt like a little oasis, a promise of peace amidst the bustling city.

When she unlocked the grand front door, a strange caution washed over her. The space seemed larger than she remembered. Was it too big? Too extravagant? She shook off the thought and began walking through the rooms, mentally arranging furniture and measuring windows for curtains.

She noted the need for rugs to add warmth and a sense of homeliness. The kitchen was basic, with a single sink, rough wooden cabinets and a marble worktop. Upstairs, she checked the bathrooms again, relieved to find the plumbing in working order.

Stepping onto the balcony, she gasped at the view of the lake. The water sparkled in the afternoon sun, and two boys fished from a small wooden boat.

Realising she'd spent over two hours there, Kate hurried back to the hut. The woman and the motorbike driver were chatting, occasionally laughing in between. Kate clasped the woman's hands, bowing slightly in gratitude.

'See you later,' she said, climbing onto the bike. As they drove away, Kate resolved to prioritize learning the language.

There was so much she wanted to understand and appreciate about her new home.

Kate hurried back to the office, her damp shoes squelching with each step. She darted into the hotel to freshen up, determined to shower, change into something more presentable and swap her soggy shoes for a dry pair. Feeling more composed, she popped back into the office to briefly catch up with Hun and Houng, expressing her heartfelt thanks for their steadfast support over the past few hectic weeks.

As she spoke, their smiles suddenly faltered. Kate turned to see the reason: her ever-present 'Policeman Follower' stood in the doorway, expressionless.

Houng, with an unusual acuity, asked the policeman what he wanted. He informed them that the English class would be held in a different building that evening and that Kate needed to be there by 5 p.m., half an hour earlier than usual.

'Oh, right. Could you please write down the new address so Mr Houng knows where to take me?' Kate replied, doing her best to maintain a polite smile despite her growing unease.

The policeman left, and as Kate prepared to leave, Hun discreetly handed her a scrap of paper. In careful, deliberate handwriting, it read: *'You will be OK, Miss Kate.'* The simple reassurance made her smile.

Ten minutes later, Mr Houng pulled up outside a large, dilapidated building. Kate hesitated, staring at its cracked facade and broken windows. The place looked utterly abandoned.

With a deep breath, she stepped inside. The air was heavy, humid and faintly metallic. The silence was oppressive, amplifying the creak of her footsteps on the warped wooden floor. A policeman from her class appeared at the end of the dimly lit corridor and gestured for her to follow. As they walked, her nerves prickled with every echo of their movements. As she walked along, she was thankful that Mr Houng was still outside and would wait for her. If there were any issues, he would go and get Stuart.

At the end of the hallway, the policeman opened a door, revealing a room alive with unexpected energy. To her astonishment, the space was packed—not only with the policemen she had taught before but also with other men of various ages. Most thrillingly, she spotted a small group of women at the back of the room, their faces laced with curious yet cautious smiles. Kate's apprehension melted into joy, and she couldn't help but beam.

At the front of the room sat the boxes of books and photo albums she had so desperately hoped to retrieve. Relief and excitement surged through her. What a day this had been— filled with challenges but also moments of triumph.

Kate quickly improvised a lesson using a cookbook she found in one of the boxes. She decided to focus on food vocabulary, translating English terms for meats and vegetables and encouraging her students to share the Vietnamese equivalents. The concept was simple but engaging, and Kate hoped it would resonate with everyone in the room.

However, just as the class was gaining momentum, the power abruptly cut out. The room was plunged into darkness, and candles were quickly lit. The lesson became disjointed, with translation mishaps and moments of confusion. Still, Kate soldiered on, buoyed by the enthusiasm of her students, especially the women who participated shyly but earnestly.

By the end of the session, Kate realised that if she wanted her lessons to be effective and enjoyable, she needed to introduce more structure and planning. A clear syllabus, interactive activities and a greater investment of her time would be crucial. She wanted her students to not only learn but also find joy and confidence in the process.

After the class, several of the men helped carry the boxes to Mr Houng's car. Kate thanked them repeatedly, using gestures to communicate her heartfelt appreciation. When she reached the small group of women, she made a point of shaking each of their hands—not with the quick formality of Western etiquette but with a lingering touch, encasing their hands in hers as a gesture of solidarity. She hoped it conveyed: *We are in this together.*

Instead of returning the boxes to the hotel, Kate called Stuart and suggested they take everything to the house. 'Brilliant idea,' Stuart replied. 'That's one less job for tomorrow.'

When they arrived at the house, they debated how best to transport the boxes without making multiple trips. To their surprise, Kate's motorbike lady offered a solution. With crates strapped to the back of her bike, she could deliver everything for the equivalent of two US dollars.

Kate, ever the doer, accepted. Perched side-saddle on the motorbike, balancing two boxes on her lap, she followed as Stuart carried additional boxes on foot.

Though they didn't linger at the house, Stuart's reaction as he stepped inside was all the reassurance Kate needed. 'It's lovely,' he said with a contented sigh. 'When you've added your personal touches, it'll feel like home. Perfect for us.'

As they locked up, Stuart added with a grin, 'Let's head back. Mr Houng deserves to get home to his family after today. And tomorrow's a big day—moving the container's contents here.'

Kate's heart leapt. 'Really? We can move in tomorrow?' Her voice rose in a high-pitched squeal of delight.

The following day, Kate was up with the sun, buzzing with excitement. After nearly four months in Vietnam, they were finally about to make the house their home. She took note to advise future clients about realistic shipping and customs timelines to manage their expectations better.

Hun and Houng had arranged for two *cyclos*—large three-wheeled bikes with passenger seating—and a small, three-wheeled van to transport the container's contents. Though Kate initially worried about the weight of the boxes and furniture, Hun assured her it was standard practice. Kate also knew it was going to mean a lot of trips, and a long day lay ahead for all of them.

With the sun setting, everything had been delivered and placed in the appropriate rooms. Exhausted but exhilarated, Kate surveyed their new home, already envisioning how she would arrange the furniture and add a personal touch.

That evening, Stuart arrived with a bottle of bubbly and a simple dinner of chicken, rice and bread. 'Sorry, it's not fancy,' he said, placing the meal on the counter. 'The champagnes from Ken and Anne—a housewarming gift.'

Kate smiled as they clinked glasses. Afterwards, she immediately rang Ken and Anne to thank them for their thoughtful housewarming gift. She expressed her excitement about inviting them over for dinner soon, eager to start repaying their boundless hospitality and support. Their encouragement had been a lifeline during this transitional phase, and Kate wanted to show her appreciation.

That night, Kate and Stuart slept soundly, their exhaustion finally succumbing to the serenity of their new surroundings.

***

The next morning, Kate and Stuart were awoken not by an alarm clock but by the gentle cacophony of nature. Ducks quacked cheerfully, hens clucked in the distance, and somewhere within the village, pigs grunted intermittently. The morning chants from the public speakers added a surreal touch to the countryside melody.

Kate opened the balcony doors, forgetting about the humidity in the air that immediately wrapped itself around her. The view was idyllic: four fishermen in their modest boats skimmed across the still lake, their rhythmic movements reflected in the shimmering water. 'Sheer bliss,' Kate exclaimed, breathing deeply and marvelling at the contrast to their previous four months here.

While their new home was far from fully functioning, Kate and Stuart embraced the challenge ahead. They both understood it would take weeks to organise everything, but that didn't deter Kate. From the beginning, she'd been methodically noting every hurdle and solution they'd encountered. Her goal was to compile a comprehensive 'Guide to Moving to Vietnam' for incoming expatriates. It would detail everything from practical advice to cultural insights.

Kate also thought of Sophie, a well-connected expatriate who was a treasure trove of local knowledge. Sophie had a knack for sourcing hard-to-find items and getting tasks done efficiently. Kate wondered if Sophie might be interested in helping new families adjust to life in Hanoi, offering services like finding homes, furniture, markets and schools for their children.

Sophie had already introduced Kate to one of her favourite local noodle cafés—a rustic gem situated on a bustling street corner. Diners sat on low stools, balancing bowls of freshly cooked noodles filled with bean sprouts, pak choi, kale and rehydrated dried mushrooms in one hand and using their chopsticks in the other. The flavours were delectable and the atmosphere authentic.

'This is fantastic,' Kate remarked, savouring the meal.

Sophie's face lit up. 'I'm glad you like it! Some newcomers aren't too keen on the simplicity, but I think it's part of the charm.'

Kate couldn't agree more. She was determined to immerse herself in these cultural experiences and embrace the authenticity of her new life.

∗∗∗

That weekend, Stuart was invited to play football with other expatriates in Hanoi. The match was in a village three hours away, and their driver, Mr Houng, was sceptical about the journey. The dirt tracks leading to the village were atrocious, riddled with potholes that turned the drive into an ordeal. The car rattled and jolted, but Kate was captivated by the scenery.

As they travelled through the countryside, she soaked up the simplicity of life around her: farmers tending to rice paddies, children playing barefoot in the fields and market vendors peddling their wares on the roadside. She snapped photo after photo, her camera capturing the unfiltered beauty of rural Vietnam.

When they finally arrived, they were stunned to find over 2,500 spectators gathered for the match. This wasn't the low-key, friendly game they had expected. The Hanoi Capitals, Stuart's team, included both semi-regular players and those simply in it for the camaraderie. They were warmly greeted by the local mayor and invited to a lavish spread of Vietnamese dishes—salads, rice and an array of fish prepared with spices that danced on the palate.

Despite Stuart scoring a goal, the team lost 3–1 to the local side. The spectators cheered good-naturedly, and the mayor extended an invitation for them to return. One of the Australian players suggested hosting a rematch in Hanoi, turning the day into a memorable cultural exchange.

Chapter 11: Of Chickens, Currencies, and Clashes

Over the next two months, life settled into a rhythm, albeit with challenges. Somehow, they managed to find old pipes and suitable adapters to create a waste pipe and water connection for the washing machine. To her horror, the first wash took nearly three hours. Kate had bought her first live chicken and watched, with sadness, as it was slaughtered and gutted for her. She had decided to cook it in the microwave for convenience – a poor decision. It took an hour and a half! It turned out that the electric voltage was only 190, while the microwave and all their electrical appliances required 240 volts. As a result, everything worked at a much slower pace. Well, that is what she told herself. She, of course, could not verify this as she was not an electrician, but it definitely took much longer than it had done back in Blighty.

They had been 'advised'—in other words, told—to employ a lady to do their cooking, cleaning and shopping. Kate resisted for months, coming up with every excuse to avoid hiring someone. She did not agree with the concept of having 'staff' in their home. It was her and Stuart's responsibility, not someone else's. Eventually, though, she had to give in.

Hun had once again helped her, along with Mr Houng, to find a suitable candidate. Miss Hoa was in her early thirties, Kate thought, and she seemed genuinely pleased to be offered the position. She had never worked for another expatriate family, but Hun was confident she would be excellent.

Over the following weeks, Kate spent hours teaching Miss Hoa how to use the Hoover, which terrified her at first: iron their shirts and operate the washing machine. Miss Hoa insisted on continuing to wash all the floors by hand on her knees, refusing even to use the mop. It was a steep learning curve for both of them, and it felt like a clash of cultures, though not in an unpleasant way. The whole arrangement didn't sit comfortably with Kate, and she struggled with it. She allowed Miss Hoa to clean, and she taught her how to shop for them at the local markets, but Kate insisted on doing all the cooking.

The following week, Kate took Miss Hoa to the markets, and they somehow muddled through haggling for produce, loosely discussing the meals for the week. Kate had also decided to show the lady at the chicken stall how to gut, cut and fillet the chicken properly so she could ask her to prepare 5 kilos of chicken and supply the carcasses for stock. It took Kate about an hour to show her. Chicken worked out to around £1.70 per kilo, with pork costing about the same. Kate had been rather apprehensive about buying pork, fearing it might contain worms, but they could only eat so much chicken, so they decided to try it. The beef, which was actually buffalo, was a complete disaster. It was as tough as old boots, even after cooking slowly overnight.

During these weeks, Kate had a revelation. She began cooking chicken and vegetables on the BBQ—quick, reliable and far tastier.

Kate found it difficult not having fresh fruit and vegetables every day. By the time she finished work and made it to the markets, the produce left looked unappetizing, and some were even rotten, which completely put her off. She decided that she needed to meet Miss Hoa at 7 am the next morning, after which her 'best friend,' the motorbike lady, would bring her back to the house before driving Kate around to meet clients. Mr Houng picked them up, took them to the market and then took Stuart to the port to clear a few containers.

They returned, and Kate, in her best Vietnamese, asked the little stallholder next to the hotel for Chicken and Rice without MSG. By now, they had gotten used to her and, thankfully, understood and prepared the dish without the dreaded MSG since Hun had spoken to them and explained that it had made Kate very ill.

With the help of Hun and Houng, they had recruited a young lady called Binh to handle all the Vietnamese accounts work. She had started a few months earlier but shocked them the previous day by announcing that she was leaving to work for the government. They had offered her 'great' opportunities, including the chance to travel. They had been paying her US$260.00 per month, but her new job would only pay US$60.00 per month. Kate wished her much happiness and success, saying that if she wasn't happy, she could always come back to them. Apparently, working for the government was the only way to obtain an international passport.

In the two weeks before Binh left, Kate and Stuart spent time with her, clearing the debts and unpaid invoices, and putting systems in place for the new person. It wouldn't make the balance sheet look good, but at least it would provide Stuart with an honest picture of cash flow and clear the historical debts that had been there before his time.

Soon, they began to find peace in their new home, enjoying the occasional escape from the ever-present demands of existing clients, prospective ones and the tight-knit diplomatic expatriate community. The evenings spent at home provided a reprieve, a chance to exhale away from prying eyes and constant scrutiny. In a community as small as theirs, news travelled faster than anyone could anticipate—whether it was good, bad, or utterly trivial.

Kate felt the pressure of maintaining a professional demeanor at all times, especially since many expatriates and diplomats were potential clients. She was acutely aware of the need to tread carefully, both in conversation and conduct. However, she and Stuart had made connections with a few individuals who felt like genuine friends, though she couldn't help but notice a clique within the community—a group tightly guarding their exclusivity. It didn't bother her; she knew where her focus needed to be.

Within the expatriate community, Kate had observed that only a select few women were willing to venture out in the evenings or participate in the Saturday 'Hash' events. For Kate and Stuart, their work required a careful balance—engagement without over-familiarity, maintaining a level of professionalism that ensured clients viewed them as trustworthy and dependable.

Stuart also faced significant challenges in his role, learning how to manage a team in a foreign country while grappling with the expectations of demanding clients. Kate recognised how steep the learning curve was for him, but she admired his resilience. Despite occasional clashes with clients who didn't take to his direct manner, Stuart had embraced the need for patience, persistence and politeness. Kate often reminded him how proud she was of what he had accomplished in such a short time.

Kate, on the other hand, had started attending evening networking events solo, as Stuart preferred to stay home. These events allowed her to channel her professional background, mingling confidently in what was often a male-dominated space. Stuart, meanwhile, took pleasure in smaller victories outside the office, such as successfully setting up their television, much to his delight.

Chapter 12: A Visitor from Home

On a Saturday 'Hash,' Kate was approached by several people who were commenting on her recent networking night. 'You really let your hair down, by all accounts,' one person teased. Another chimed in, 'Didn't know you could jive like that, Kate!' Stuart, unfazed, simply smiled. He trusted her completely and knew she could hold her own. Her past experiences in hotel management had given her the confidence and ability to navigate any social situation.

With every passing month, Kate's English classes were proving to be a surprising success. She had spent hours carefully planning structured lessons, and more women from the local community had begun attending. Even the Commander's wife had joined, an honour that boosted Kate's morale. The classes weren't just about language; they became a meeting ground where women from different backgrounds connected.

To encourage participation, Kate introduced games that required men and women to collaborate to form sentences and describe words. Initially, the men resisted working alongside the women, but the latter shone brightly, proving themselves a force to be reckoned with. What touched Kate most was the presence of children at the lessons. Their wide-eyed enthusiasm and sparkling excitement seemed to inspire the adults as well.

Kate's early experiences with a local 'hairdresser' were unforgettable. She vividly recalled her first visit, where a makeshift salon on a dusty roadside became the setting for an unexpected moment of serenity. A woman had sprinkled some kind of powder into Kate's hair before proceeding to massage her scalp. Despite her initial scepticism, the experience turned out to be incredibly relaxing. She closed her eyes, forgetting her surroundings entirely.

Several months later, Sophie introduced her to a 'proper' hairdressing salon run by a Vietnamese woman with a French father. The salon was a perfect blend of Western influence and Vietnamese charm. Kate crossed her fingers as they prepared to wash her hair, and to her delight, the scalp massage was as exquisite as she had hoped. This discovery was a small yet significant win, one she was eager to share in the newsletter for expatriates.

Nevertheless, she felt pangs of homesickness, albeit occasionally. When Mark and Scott sent her photos of their vibrant garden back home, she couldn't help but long for the familiar sights and smells. Mark had transformed the garage wall into a backdrop for a stunning yellow rose bush, adding trellises for support.

Kate laughed as she remembered her own poor attempts at caring for indoor plants. 'When did you last water these?' Mark had asked, only to be met with Kate's sheepish admission: 'A couple of months ago, maybe?' Her nonchalant approach to gardening had been a running joke. Ultimately, she had happily handed over her plants to Mark and Scott, knowing they would thrive under better care.

****

Kate and Stuart had recently discovered that a new 'Western-style' restaurant had opened nearby, featuring live performances by a local jazz band twice a week. Intrigued, they decided to pay a visit. The restaurant, with its warm lighting and cosy decor, exuded a lively yet sophisticated charm. As they dined, they struck up a conversation with the owner, a wealthy Vietnamese gentleman with an extraordinary story. He had spent years living in Cuba, only returning to Vietnam when he felt it was safe. Now, he was not only a restaurateur but also the proud owner of seven expansive 'Western-style' properties in the affluent Westlake area, generating substantial income in US dollars.

After some time, the owner joined them at their table. He was gracious and personable, offering Kate an unexpected proposition: part-time work helping him market his restaurant and improve its overall operations. The offer came with a generous pay of $700 per month. While flattered, Kate politely declined. Her commitments to her primary job and the English classes she taught for the local police and community left her with no spare time.

As they prepared to leave, cycling home under a canopy of stars, the guard at the restaurant commented, 'It's been raining dogs and cats!' Both Kate and Stuart burst out laughing, amused by his endearing mix-up, and chose not to correct him.

One thing that deeply upset Kate was the knowledge that most of the letters and handmade cards she had carefully sent over the past two years had never reached their destinations in the UK or Spain. The effort she had put into crafting each one—ensuring the content was polite and devoid of any critique of Vietnam's communist society—made the loss all the more frustrating. Determined to uncover the reason, she resolved to investigate whether her correspondence was being intercepted or held somewhere. If they could be retrieved, she hoped to give them to her mum to take back to the UK and post directly to her family and friends. Kate was so excited that her mum was visiting her the next week.

September 1996

Kate stood at the arrival terminal of Hanoi airport, excitement and apprehension bubbling inside her. The airport, with its bucolic charm and chaotic energy, felt familiar after two years of regular visits, and many of the staff recognized her.

'Mum! mum, over here!' Kate called, waving enthusiastically.

As her mother emerged from the crowd, Kate wrapped her arms around her, hugging her tightly. Relief washed over her—her mum had arrived safely after the long journey.

'It's so good to finally be here and see where you live,' her mum said, happy but exhausted.

Kate had carefully planned the next three weeks to mix business with pleasure. Together, they would travel across Vietnam and even make a trip to Bangkok, combining work commitments with opportunities to explore and create memories. Mr Houng greeted Kate's mum with a wide smile and shook her hand before taking them to the village.

Back at Nghi Tam Village, Kate's Motorbike Taxi lady greeted them warmly and made a mischievous offer.

'Would you like to ride side-saddle on my motorbike to the house?' she asked Kate's mum in broken English.

Her mother shot Kate a questioning look. 'You're joking, right?'

'No joke, mum! This is just the beginning of your adventure,' Kate replied with a grin.

Eventually, her mum opted for the safety of walking, much to everyone's amusement. Once home, Kate suggested a quick change into shorts, a T-shirt and trainers for their first outing. Despite her mother's initial protests, Kate insisted they head to the local Hash House Harriers run.

'You need to stay awake until at least 9 pm, Mum. This, plus what we have arranged for the evening, will help. Trust me, you will thank me honestly,' Kate said with a broad smile.

The setting for the Hash was breathtaking. Surrounded by verdant 'paddy fields' and towering trees, with water buffalo grazing nearby, the vibrant countryside was in contradiction to the hustle and bustle of Hanoi. Kate's mum, though initially hesitant, soon found herself laughing and chatting with the other participants, even as her trainers squelched through mud and water reached her knees.

Camera in hand, Kate was determined to make the most of her time with her mother and create magical memories for both of them. Her mum had been warmly welcomed, and although she had grumbled while walking and jogging through the paddy fields, with the water rising above her knees, the mud squelching between her toes, and her cheeks flushed from the exhaustion and heat, a big smile was now on her face. She was laughing with some of the other hashers beside her.

Kate's mum got her own back later in the Hash circle, where she had the privilege of pouring a large jug of beer over

Kate and making her do a 'down down' as her forfeit. Fortunately, her mum had avoided the dreaded 'new shoes' forfeit, much to Kate's relief.

The group's infectious energy set the tone for a memorable evening, capped off by seeing dozens of villagers gathered around a local person's hut, trying to get a glimpse of the large television screen to watch an international football match. The atmosphere was electric, with cheers and laughter filling the air. Kate could not quite get her head round the fact that there were wires everywhere, a generator to charge the electric cable and somehow a signal – all from this small hut made of bamboo.

Kate's mum, wide-eyed, took in the surroundings, but a smile spread across her face at the scene before her.

The evening was thoroughly enjoyable, and Kate took her mum home at 9 pm. She settled her in, and her mum slept like a log that night.

Chapter 13: The Ride of a Lifetime

The following morning, Kate took a cup of tea up to her mum, who was sitting on the balcony, gazing out at the lake.

'Ah, Kate, this is glorious—what a view. Thank you for the tea. I was so annoyed with you dragging me out when I first arrived yesterday, but now I understand why you were determined to keep me awake,' her mum said, beaming with a big smile.

They embraced, then sat together on the balcony, chatting for hours.

Over the following days, Kate introduced her mum to Miss Hoa, the ladies in the office and took her out to explore the markets, street stalls and the noodle stall that Sophie had introduced her to. She also booked a visit to the dressmaker and introduced her to some of their friends. Kate was pleasantly surprised to find that, after the initial few days, they were both relaxed, happy and affectionate in each other's company—despite hardly spending any time together over the past fifteen years.

Kate had planned for her mum to experience as much as possible during her holiday, including a visit to her street hairdresser, as well as a trip to the lovely French-Vietnamese hair salon, among other things.

The following Monday, Mr Houng took them both to the airport, and they flew south to Da Nang. The airport was a reminder of what Hanoi used to be like. Her mum chuckled at seeing locals carrying live ducks as hand luggage, their heads sticking out from the baskets, and at the chaotic scene of people boarding the plane. She said it felt like a lucky dip whether you got a seat or not, as there was no seat allocation.

Da Nang, a central hub for three world cultural heritages—Hue Ancient Town, Hoi An Ancient Town, and My Son Sanctuary—is also one of the most important shipping ports for importing and exporting Vietnamese products. Surrounded by mountains to the west and the South China Sea to the east, with the Han River flowing through the centre of the city, it was a fascinating place to visit.

Kate had arranged for two motorbikes to meet them at the airport and take them to a village on the way to Hoi An. Her mum stared in disbelief at Kate.

'You think I'm getting on the back of that motorbike? You've got another thing coming,' she said, her cheeks flushed with rage and astonishment.

'Mum, it's the only way we can get around. Trust me, you'll be safe, I promise. Just hold onto the driver's waist, and I'll be behind you on the other motorbike, doing the same,' Kate reassured her, placing her mum's bag over her shoulder alongside the small rucksack she already had on her back.

The roads were busy, rough, dusty and dirty. The noise was deafening, with lorries and other vehicles everywhere, but it wasn't dangerous. Kate would never have put her mum through this if it were. They arrived at the village, and Kate helped her mum off the bike.

'My bum is totally numb, Kate. I had my eyes closed the whole way,' her mum complained.

'Mum, come this way and stretch your legs. We're going to a pottery factory; they're expecting us,' Kate said, gently guiding her mum across the path and handing her a bottle of water to drink as they walked.

The pottery was renowned for exporting its products all over the world, and Kate had a meeting to discuss the possibility of managing their shipping requirements.

Both Kate and her mum were amazed to see that the workforce was made up almost entirely of women, with only three men overseeing the manufacturing. They were particularly intrigued by the fact that most of the women operating the tabletop potter's wheels were also pressing a wooden pedal with their right foot simultaneously. Other women sat on very low stools, operating other potter's wheels underneath the table of the main wheel, and in some cases, young children were sitting on stools, pressing the foot pedal to operate the wheels. One woman was providing power to two potter's tables by pressing the pedal consistently with her right foot. It was unbelievable and incredibly exhausting, Kate thought, while her mum was shocked by the sight. There must have been at least fifty of these tables, surrounded by benches where other women were carving, packing or labelling the items. So much detail went into the plant pots, containers, tableware and jugs.

It was a real eye-opener for Kate's mum, who was totally absorbed in it all. Kate knew that the conversation ahead would be lengthy, but she was relieved to see her mum so engrossed.

As Kate turned to say, 'See you soon, mum,' she saw that one of the women had taken her mum's hand and led her to a table, where it looked like she was going to have a go on the potter's wheel.

Just under two hours later, Kate emerged, smiling. Her meeting had been a great success, securing several 20-foot containers of products to be shipped to various parts of the world. The HCMC office would manage it, as they were closer and knew the local customs and port officials.

Kate went over to her mum, who was still working the potter's wheel, making what looked like a vase. She was completely consumed by the process. Kate couldn't help but smile; it was wonderful seeing her mum so happy, and somehow, she and the Vietnamese woman were communicating freely. Kate sat a little distance away, watching with pleasure as her mum finished her piece of art.

'Oh, hi!' her mother exclaimed, turning away from the pottery wheel as she noticed Kate standing nearby.

'Hi, mum. Your vases look incredible! Have you been working at the wheel all this time?' Kate asked, her voice filled with admiration.

'Oh, how long has it been? I've completely lost track. Look!' Her mother gestured enthusiastically to a set of four vases, each of varying sizes. 'I've made a whole set. They still need to be fired in the kiln, though,' she added, her eyes sparkling with pure joy.

'No problem at all. They can be fired while we're travelling, and we can collect them on the way back,' Kate replied reassuringly. 'I'll go and settle the bill for the kiln firing now. Honestly, Mum, they're stunning. I love the detail you've put into them.'

Her mother beamed. 'How much did they cost, Kate?' she asked curiously as they climbed onto their respective motorbikes.

'All sorted, mum. But for your information, they were so inexpensive that I might even look into exporting a few to have back home,' Kate replied with a grin. 'Now, hold on tight—we're off to Hoi An!'

The motorbike ride to Hoi An was exhilarating for Kate, as always. The warm air rushed past, carrying with it the scents of the countryside—earthy fields, blossoming flowers and an occasional hint of wood smoke. To her delight, Kate noticed her mother was finally relaxing and taking in the scenery this time rather than riding with her eyes squeezed shut. The vivid green rice paddies stretched out on either side of the road, dotted with water buffalo grazing lazily, their tails swishing in the sun. The occasional cyclist or motorbike passed by, but the ride was largely peaceful, the road unfolding like a ribbon ahead of them.

Hoi An, an ancient and remarkably well-preserved city on Vietnam's central coast, awaited them with its unique charm. The city's architectural scene was a mesmerizing concoction of eras and styles—brightly coloured temples, Chinese shophouses with intricate wood carvings, narrow Vietnamese tube houses and elegant French colonial buildings. Kate had always been fascinated by the iconic Japanese Covered Bridge, with its delicate pagoda sitting atop, serving as the city's historical ties with Japan.

On a previous visit, Kate had learned of a fascinating discovery near the Cham Islands, just off Hoi An's coast. In 1996, a team of businessmen began excavating a shipwreck and recovered over 250,000 ceramic artefacts, including beautifully crafted tableware. Many of these treasures were now housed in Hanoi's National Collection Centre. Hoi An, once a busy trading port between Vietnam, China, and Japan from the 15th to the 19th centuries, eventually shifted its focus to fishing and vibrant markets when its maritime significance waned.

Arriving at the 'hotel,' a term Kate used loosely, they were greeted warmly by the family who owned the home. She had stumbled upon this gem on her first business trip to Hoi An and had chosen to stay there every visit since. The house was modest but delightful, its location a dream—just ten metres from the water's edge.

Kate loved the serene rhythm of life there. She often watched women returning from the river, their baskets brimming with freshly caught fish, which they carefully prepared for the market just a stone's throw away. Wooden huts on stilts lined the Thu Bon River, their reflections shimmering in the water. Narrowboats were tied to the stilts, with makeshift rope ladders providing access. Men, women and children bustled about in conical hats, a handful sporting the odd Western-style flat cap. The conical hats, however, were far more practical—providing complete protection from the sun and doubling as waterproof shields during sudden downpours.

The market itself was lively and sensory overload. The air was filled with the earthy scent of clay and mud underfoot, mixed with the aroma of fresh produce and spices. Ducks, hens, and even a few scruffy dogs wandered freely, always returning to their owners when needed. Kate was intrigued at the contrast between the plastic crates used by some vendors and the fragile structures of the stalls themselves, which were held together with bamboo poles, palm tree trunks and roofs patched with banana leaves or bits of plastic.

The sights never ceased to astonish her. Once, she had seen a pot-bellied pig sprawled across the petrol tank of a motorbike while the driver's wife perched behind him, cradling another pig in her arms. Behind them, a child stood unsteadily on the back of the seat, clutching his mother's neck. Kate had wished she could capture the moment in a photo, but riding sidesaddle on her own motorbike had made it impossible.

Despite the charm, certain aspects of Vietnamese culture were difficult for her to reconcile. Dog meat remained a common delicacy, and Kate had often seen crates of live dogs strapped to the backs of motorbikes destined for market. Though it saddened her, she reminded herself that she was a guest in their world and had to respect their traditions.

The memory of her first visit to the snake markets near Hanoi came to mind, sending a shiver down her spine. Le Mat, the Snake Village, was infamous for its snake restaurants, and Kate had been both horrified and fascinated. She vividly recalled her visit to the dimly lit restaurant, where she and Stuart had been asked to choose a live snake to eat. The memory of the glass tank writhing with serpents made her skin crawl even now. Yet, she had faced the experience with as much dignity as she could muster, determined to embrace the culture despite her fears.

The memory took her back to the relentless invitations and requests during her and Stuart's first year in Vietnam to visit a snake restaurant. Locals considered it an honour to be invited, but the very thought filled Kate with dread. She had been petrified of snakes since childhood, haunted by recurring nightmares of snakes writhing across her bedroom floor. Growing up, it hadn't helped that her father's uncle's garden was a haven for adders and grass snakes. Those visits were supposed to be about riding Kerry, a beautiful black horse with a white streak down the centre of her face. She adored, but even then, her joy was shadowed by the lurking fear of encountering a snake.

Her father's tennis matches there were equally memorable—though not for his skills on the court. He flatly refused to cross to the other side of the net, worried that a snake might slither out unexpectedly. Looking back, it seemed absurd, but those childhood fears lingered, shaping her hesitation as an adult.

Eventually, Kate mustered the courage to visit Le Mat, the Snake Village. It was, quite literally, a village dedicated to snakes, located just outside Hanoi near Viet Hung province. The place was a hub of activity, with Kate estimating nearly a hundred market stalls, all selling snakes of various types and sizes. To her horror, the wooden crates used to house the snakes had gaps that looked far too large for comfort. All she could think about was what might be slithering beneath the benches, out of sight. Even the memory made her shiver. Despite her trepidation, she couldn't deny it was a highly lucrative trade, and the locals were proud of their reputation.

It wasn't until just before her mother arrived that Kate and Stuart finally agreed to visit a snake restaurant. They decided to 'get it over with' as diplomatically as possible. The restaurant in Le Mat was dimly lit, with a faintly musty smell that clung to the air. The moment they entered, Kate's eyes were drawn to a large glass tank ahead. It was filled with snakes, their coiled bodies gleaming under the low light. As they approached, the restaurant manager greeted them and invited them to choose a snake for their meal.

Panic surged through Kate as she turned to Jean-Pierre, one of their dining companions, for support. 'I have no idea, Jean-Pierre,' she said, her voice shaking. 'Can you please take control of this? I can't even bear to look at them, let alone choose one to eat.'

Jean-Pierre had been an anchor for Kate and Stuart since their arrival in Vietnam. A towering figure with a gentle demeanour, he was a veteran of the Vietnam War who had returned years later to lend his expertise. He was as diplomatic as he was knowledgeable, and his calm authority had been a godsend during the more challenging moments of their time in the country.

Jean-Pierre selected a snake, and the manager used a long stick with a hook to extract it from the tank. As the snake's body writhed around the hook, the other snakes in the tank became restless, sliding up towards the top edge of the glass. Instinctively, Kate took a step back, gripping the nearest table for support.

The manager, holding the snake high, invited the group to follow him to their table. Kate made sure to position herself as far away from the snake as possible, ensuring she couldn't see the tank either. She was trying to maintain her composure when, to her horror, the manager pulled out a knife and slit the snake just below its jaw, cutting down about six inches. As the blood began to flow, he turned the snake upside down and held it over a large glass jug, squeezing out the remaining blood with practised precision.

The blood was poured into small glasses and distributed among the group. Jean-Pierre and the others drank theirs effortlessly, as if it were a casual shot of vodka. Kate, however, froze, the warm glass in her hand emitting a metallic scent that made her stomach churn. She couldn't say how she stopped herself from being sick at the table. With a deep breath and a monumental effort of will, she managed to take the smallest sip, just enough to avoid offending their Vietnamese hosts.

The next ordeal came when a waiter presented what looked like a heart. It was offered to Stuart, who immediately turned to Kate for reassurance. She whispered, 'Don't if you don't want to.' Sensing his hesitation, Jean-Pierre stepped in, consuming the heart with a surprising elegance that seemed to diffuse the tension. Kate clasped her hands in gratitude and mouthed, 'Thank you' to him, relieved that he had taken charge.

The heart and liver, they were told, were considered potent medicines that were believed to enhance male fertility. Despite her initial revulsion, Kate was shocked to find that she actually enjoyed the snake meat itself. It was tender and richly flavoured, akin to a particularly succulent chicken breast. Reflecting on the experience later, she realized it was one of the most bizarre and memorable meals of her life.

'Kate, you alright?' Her mum tugged at her arm as she asked, pulling her out of nostalgia.

'Oh yes, mum, sorry. Seeing the snakes in the market just brought back that awful, lingering memory of when Stuart and I went to the Snake Restaurant. Apologies. Come on, let's go and enjoy some freshly caught king-size prawns, coriander leaf salad and rice,' Kate said, hugging her mum.

Her mum was in her element, relishing the fresh fish. The prawns were succulent and juicy, so tender they seemed to melt in your mouth, yet still 'fleshy' in texture. The sharpness of the coriander salad cleared the palate.

That afternoon, Kate had arranged for her and her mum to take a ride across the river, through the fields, past the small hamlet dwellings, and back around Hoi An city, along its waterways to the Japanese Bridge. The 'hotel' had lent them the bikes. Kate had jokingly called them 'sit-up-and-beg bikes.' The hard, narrow saddles were positioned quite high, the handlebars even higher, and the only method of braking was scraping your feet along the floor, hoping it would slow you down. Just getting onto the bikes had them both in fits of laughter. They had also taken a narrow fishing boat down the canals, and Kate did her best to engage with the lady rowing them.

Later, they returned to their respective motorbikes, and the drivers took them to a local beach. It was pristine. The waves glistened, the sand was soft underfoot, and the water was warm as they paddled. It felt untouched by Western influences, with only a few small wooden huts nestled into the dunes dotted along the coastline.

Fishermen were in boats lined up in rows, casting and hauling large nets in unison, while women sold *bánh mì* in the village streets, and small stallholders offered fresh fruit and vegetables. They stopped to purchase some items and savoured the flavours together.

In the evening, Kate had organised a boat ride under the moonlight. The Vietnamese tradition was to light a lantern, make a wish, and set it afloat on the river. The evening felt magical and made Kate feel quite spiritual. The air was warm but not too humid, the river was still, and the sky was clear, with stars shining brightly.

The next day, Kate had planned to take her mum to Hue, but the journey was nearly 120 kilometres long, and she thought it might be a bit much for her mum on the back of a motorbike. It was a shame, as Hue was a beautiful ancient city steeped in history with stunning architecture. However, common sense prevailed. Perhaps on her next visit—if there was to be one.

Hue's Imperial City was home to hundreds of monuments dating back to the early 19th century, including the Royal Tombs, temples, the Forbidden Purple City and the Royal Quarters. The city was set along the northern bank of the Perfume River.

The journey back to Da Nang Airport was bumpy, noisy and dusty. The only positive, from her mum's perspective, was collecting her four vases from the pottery.

Upon returning to Hanoi and their home, Kate and her mum had just stepped inside when the heavens opened. Thankfully, they hadn't been caught in the rain. The storm was torrential, and once again, water poured through the windows from the top floor, cascading down to the ground on the east side of their home. It ran down the staircase and flooded the main dining room/lounge. It had happened many times since they'd moved in, but never quite as badly as that particular day.

Together, they mopped up the water and dried the stairs. Kate had learned to live with it and not let it get to her. Her main priority was her mum's safety.

Kate had taken her mum to Mrs Wang, the dressmaker, when she first arrived, and by the time they returned to Hanoi, the clothes were ready for a fitting. It gave her mum peace of mind, and Kate had complete confidence the clothing would fit perfectly. Her mum was over the moon with how the clothes looked and felt. It was a result Kate was proud of, and it made her happy to see the genuine smile on her mum's face.

They were all due to fly to Bangkok two days later. Kate was going to show her mum around for a few days while Stuart visited the partner office and arranged for their Vietnamese visas to be renewed. After that, they would all take a break at Hau Hin, a stunning new resort just outside Bangkok. Only an hour's drive away, it was an understated resort offering exceptional service and peacefulness. Kate could see herself and Stuart visiting frequently when they needed to escape Vietnam.

The 100% humidity, temperatures exceeding 30°C, and constant walking were starting to take their toll on her mum. But despite her exhaustion, her mum was determined to enjoy all the experiences Kate had planned for her. She knew that a few days at the resort would provide the rest she needed before flying home, and she planned to soak up as much of Bangkok as she could.

Saying 'See you soon' to her mum at Bangkok Airport was harder than she had imagined. They both found themselves in tears, reluctant to let go of each other at the departure gate. Neither had expected the bond they would share after the initial few days of adjusting. It was a new chapter in their relationship, Kate thought, with a warm feeling inside her.

Stuart and Kate flew back to Hanoi an hour later, and Kate immediately slipped back into the realities of work mode.

Chapter 14: Hanoi to Ha Long Bay

Liz arrived a month after Kate's mum's departure. Expectedly, she quickly immersed herself in the day-to-day living experiences of Hanoi. She delighted in having bespoke clothes made, each garment fitting her perfectly and making her feel truly special. She had brought an empty suitcase with her, determined to fill it with a new wardrobe of tailored outfits.

Liz accompanied Kate and Miss Hoa to the numerous bustling markets and street stalls where they sourced their monthly provisions. On one occasion, while helping to wash an assortment of fruit, salad greens and vegetables, Liz was taken aback to see Kate using washing-up liquid during the process.

'It's a must,' Kate explained matter-of-factly, 'to ensure all the bugs are removed and everything is thoroughly disinfected.'

A particularly thrilling discovery at the market was a cauliflower—an absolute rarity in Hanoi. It felt like a true culinary treat. Liz later joined Kate on a trip to Ho Chi Minh City (HCMC) for two weeks of meetings and business development. While there, Kate had heard through the grapevine that lamb, her favourite meat, was now available in one of the shops. The news was met with considerable excitement.

Liz and Kate returned just in time for the Saturday Hash, a significant event as Kate and Stuart were hosting it. Ken, along with a few other friends, had helped Stuart set the route, while Kate had arranged for custom T-shirts to be printed for the Hashers. These T-shirts featured their Hash names and fitting illustrations on the front, and on the back bore the slogan, *'Enjoy a Moving Experience.'* Beneath it were footprints, accompanied by the phrase, *'Moving the People, Making the Difference.'*

Unfortunately, torrential rain earlier that morning had washed away the original trail, forcing Stuart and Ken to re-lay the route using another 15 kilos of flour.

The effort paid off. An impressive 122 people turned up, an overwhelming but rewarding turnout given the earlier downpour. Liz thoroughly enjoyed the Hash, which featured a well-planned route with numerous false trails that led participants through paddy fields, quaint villages and even onto a narrow boat across a river—only to have to turn back.

Liz earned her customary 'visitor's down-down' (a traditional Hash drinking forfeit) with good humour.

Kate and Stuart had also grown particularly close to an Australian couple they'd met in Hanoi. Slightly older, the pair were a constant source of great company and laughter. They often joined Kate and Stuart on adventures, including the occasional Hash or mountain biking excursion. Their friendship was rock-solid, and Kate held them in the highest regard.

Rosie, the wife, was a strong, inspirational and fiercely independent woman who taught at the International School while her husband, a quantity surveyor, was managing two major projects in Hanoi. Kate admired their grounded nature, sense of fun and zest for life. She felt certain that their friendship would endure, no matter where life took them.

After spending their first eighteen months in Hanoi with no visitors, Kate and Stuart suddenly found themselves hosting a stream of friends and family. Three weeks after Liz's departure, more friends arrived, and they had planned a trip to Ha Long Bay as a brief escape. While Kate and Stuart sincerely appreciated the effort made by loved ones to visit them in such an unfamiliar part of the world, they had to juggle these visits with the demands of their work, ensuring they stayed ahead of their competitors and maintained the hard-earned market share they had worked tirelessly to secure. It was a constant balancing act—difficult to avoid feeling guilty about not spending more time with visitors while staying focused on their professional responsibilities.

The journey to Ha Long Bay from Hanoi, a mere 165 kilometres, was an adventure in itself. Transporting six adults there in 1996 posed a logistical challenge. Kate decided they would travel via Hai Phong along what the Vietnamese officials optimistically referred to as Highway Five. In reality, it was a bumpy, rough dirt track devoid of lighting or road markings.

The 'highway' was alive with chaos: inexperienced lorry drivers in decrepit, second-hand vehicles; buses overloaded with hessian sacks, bicycles and crates of animals—ducks, hens and even dogs: motorbikes, cyclists and the occasional farmer urging his cattle across the road added to the pandemonium.

The two-and-a-half-hour journey was a test of nerves, punctuated by gasps, screams and horrified expressions from their friends. Yet, in retrospect, the sheer unpredictability of the ride became part of the adventure—a memorable prelude to their Ha Long Bay getaway.

Haiphong, located in north-eastern Vietnam across from Cat Ba Island, was originally the homeland of Lê Chân, a female general who heroically resisted Chinese domination in 40 AD. She is credited with establishing *Hải Tần Phòng Thủ*, which translates to 'Defended Sea Coast.' The French later left a significant mark on the region, establishing a joint tax agency with the Nguyễn Dynasty in 1874 to manage and develop trade. They also set up a naval base, further cementing their influence. Over time, Haiphong evolved into a major industrial hub renowned for its production of cement, fish-canning and numerous large shipyards.

The city itself boasts wide boulevards lined with landmarks from the French colonial era. Notable examples include the elegant opera house, the extraordinary Buddhist *Du Hang Pagoda*, and the Queen of the Rosary Cathedral, which dates back to the early 19th century. These monuments give the city a rich and distinct cultural character.

Kate had waved off their friends on two rather precarious-looking cyclos—essentially bicycles fitted with wooden-framed seats at the front, complete with a raised section for feet and two small stabilising wheels on either side. A snug fit for two Western bodies, the contraptions were pedalled by local men and women. To ensure their friends wouldn't get lost, Kate handed the drivers a piece of paper with instructions written in Vietnamese, carefully outlining the return time and location. This arrangement kept their guests entertained for a few hours, allowing Stuart to meet with customs officials to clear clients' shipping containers. They then visited two prospective clients setting up businesses in Haiphong, eager to discuss the logistics of bringing in expatriates.

Later, Kate and Stuart took their friends to a trusted local restaurant, deliberately keeping the menu a surprise. It featured an array of local delicacies, accompanied by plenty of beer to wash it all down. By the end of the meal, everyone was thoroughly relaxed, the adventurous dining experience adding to the day's charm.

The group headed to Ha Long Bay later that day. Situated in the Gulf of Tonkin, Ha Long Bay was an ideal destination at this time of year. It comprises over 3,000 islands, with limestone mountains, caves and grottos scattered across its emerald-green waters. Sandy beaches abound, and the mild temperatures make it perfect for fishing and unwinding—a prospect Kate found irresistible.

Upon arrival, they made their way to the fishing port, where Kate used her charm and bartering skills to secure a local fisherman's boat for their adventure. It was a rustic, no-frills vessel, far from luxurious, but Kate loved its authenticity. Her friends, however, eyed it with some scepticism, questioning whether it was even seaworthy.

The excursion turned out to be an unforgettable experience. They caught an assortment of fish, including vibrant prawns, and watched as the fisherman expertly cooked their catch on the boat. He navigated them through grottos, past the entrances of majestic caves, and wove between the islands, giving them a glimpse of the many floating fishing villages nestled in the bay. As the day progressed, the fisherman offered to drop each couple off on their own private island for a few hours.

For Kate, a romantic at heart, this was pure bliss. Stuart, however, felt uneasy about being left on an island.

'How do we know he'll come back to collect us?' he asked, clearly apprehensive.

'We haven't paid him yet,' Kate replied confidently.

In the end, Stuart conceded that the experience was extraordinary. Their friends described it as magical, recounting their favourite moments with infectious enthusiasm on the boat ride back to the port.

They spent the night on the boat, rising early the next day to begin the drive back to Hanoi. Along the way, they stopped to stroll through rice fields, purchased fresh fruit from a local market and enjoyed green tea in a small roadside café, savouring the simplicity of the experience.

The group had collectively covered the cost of the trip, which included the fisherman's time, food, drinks, overnight accommodation and, of course, the freshly caught seafood. Kate handed the fisherman the equivalent of US$50—double the amount Hun had advised her to pay. For less than US$9 per person, it was worth every penny. As she shook the fisherman's hand to thank him, he held on, overwhelmed by their gratitude.

That Saturday, Kate and Stuart took their friends to the Hash, which proved just as enjoyable. The run was set in a picturesque location, and the post-Hash festivities—a lively barbecue in Kate and Stuart's garden—offered plenty of laughter and camaraderie.

On a Monday, Kate accompanied her friends to the airport, and as they prepared to depart, she couldn't hold back a few tears. Just as with Liz and her mum, she knew she would miss their laughter and company dearly. She felt a deep sense of gratitude for the effort they had made to travel all the way to Vietnam to see them.

Chapter 15: A Season of Transition

With Christmas fast approaching, Kate found herself wondering what they would do this year. She and Stuart hadn't even discussed plans yet. It was a hectic season in their industry, with clients moving into Vietnam and others packing up to relocate to new posts or jobs abroad for the New Year. There was no chance of escaping for even a few days, let alone a proper holiday.

Kate's thoughts drifted to their first Christmas in Vietnam, which felt like a lifetime ago. That year, they had decided to organise a Hash run on Christmas morning. Both Kate and Stuart had set the route and laid the flour early that day before the run. Although only seventeen people turned up, the event had been a success, with everyone showing genuine appreciation for their effort—particularly since they had sacrificed their Christmas morning to arrange it.

Later that day, Kate managed to secure a table at the only hotel in Hanoi offering a Christmas lunch. She and Stuart enjoyed a leisurely meal, complete with plenty of bubbly and laughter, alongside four close friends who were also staying in Hanoi for the holidays. Most expatriates either went on holiday or travelled home for Christmas, leaving very few in the city. While Hanoi's winter brought a biting dampness, there was no snow or frost—just a cold, heavy moisture hanging in the air.

Walking back to the office, Kate found herself laughing aloud at a memory of Sophie's young children during their first Christmas in Vietnam. She had jokingly told Freddie, with the help of his sister Florence, to lay a cord from their home in

Hanoi to wherever they would be staying that Christmas so Santa could find them. She explained that the cord would guide Santa, even through the airport and into the hotel corridors if needed.

Sophie had fully embraced the idea, adapting it to suit their travels. She switched the cord for coloured stickers, explaining to Freddie that she didn't want Santa to trip over a cord. The airline crew played along, letting Freddie place stickers on nearly all the seats of the aeroplane. When they reached their hotel, he continued placing stickers from the front door to their room and onto his bed. Kate had been delighted and thanked Sophie for supporting the whimsical tradition.

She later included the story in her December newsletter, which she sent to expats in Vietnam as well as her company's partner agents and offices around the world. The light-hearted tale was intended to spread some festive cheer, and Kate hoped other families might adopt the idea for their own children.

When Freddie and Florence returned to Vietnam in January, Kate eagerly asked if Santa had managed to find them. Freddie's face lit up with a massive grin as he nodded eagerly, showing Kate some of his presents.

From the outset, Kate had made a point of ensuring her newsletters addressed the challenges faced by families relocating to Vietnam, particularly children. She dedicated sections to their unique needs, offering detailed action plans and guidance in her *Guide to Moving to Vietnam*. Through her experiences, she had realised how often children were the forgotten ones during relocations. Parents frequently underestimated the impact on their children, assuming they would adapt quickly to new surroundings and the upheaval of leaving behind grandparents, cousins, friends, teachers, football clubs and their familiar home environment.

Similarly, Kate was mindful of the struggles faced by 'trailing spouses.' She always included advice and tips to support them in adjusting to a new country and navigating the disruption to their lives. For expatriates relocating for work, the transition was often smoother. They had the support of an established professional network and colleagues, even if they were in different countries. By contrast, trailing spouses could feel isolated, especially if they had given up a successful career or fulfilling job they couldn't continue in their new location.

As soon as Kate received details of new inbound clients, she reached out to provide her *Moving to Vietnam Guide*. She also included a short questionnaire for the trailing spouse to identify their interests and needs. Using this information, Kate could recommend local organisations, charities or networking groups in Hanoi or Ho Chi Minh City, as well as upcoming events they might wish to attend. She believed this demonstrated a sense of normality and reassurance, helping clients feel less apprehensive about their move.

Kate took pride in ensuring her clients felt supported during what could be a daunting transition. By addressing the needs of the whole family—not just the working expatriate— she believed she was making a meaningful difference.

Kate had received an abundance of positive feedback from clients regarding her observations and recommendations. She was confident that emphasising the philosophy of moving *people and their livelihoods*, rather than just furniture, was the key to their success. This approach undoubtedly helped secure numerous new clients and facilitated countless relocations, both into and out of Vietnam.

In their first year, they had the market to themselves, but competition soon emerged as two other companies entered the Vietnamese market, eager to claim a share. Despite this, Kate was immensely proud that she and Stuart had managed to secure over 85% of the moves into and out of Vietnam over the past three years. Reputation, honesty and reliability were their cornerstones, bolstered by scrupulous attention to detail for every client.

Their company's motto, featured prominently in all marketing materials, was *'Moving the People, Making the Difference,'* accompanied by an image of an adult's hand gently holding a baby's hand.

Kate had even sought Sophie and her husband Tom's permission to photograph Florence holding her teddy bear for the cover of their company brochure. The back cover displayed a thoughtful collage of personal items: a set of golf clubs, a bicycle, a picture frame, a book and a few other treasured belongings. For Kate, moving was not about transporting furniture but about relocating people's lives— their personal effects, prized possessions and homes. It was about ensuring a smooth and supported transition once they arrived in their new country.

Stuart had worked tirelessly to secure a new location for the company warehouse, overcoming logistical challenges with patience and persistence. The improved facility offered more space and better quality, positioning the business for future growth.

Kate and Stuart had developed a productive routine and rhythm in their work, and the business was thriving. Their client base spanned various industries, including hotels, sugar producers, telecommunications companies and manufacturers of food and household goods such as OMO laundry detergent, toothpaste, fizzy drinks and toiletries. Diplomatic moves also made up a significant portion of their portfolio.

Kate smiled as she recalled a conversation with a UK-based client before leaving for Vietnam. She had joked with them about the possibility of relocating their ice cream manufacturing operations to Vietnam and, if they did, asked for the honour of shipping their equipment and managing the senior management relocations. To her delight, in 1995, they followed through and awarded her the contract. Their ice cream was sold on tricycles equipped with cold boxes in Ho Chi Minh City—a quirky and satisfying success story.

The company's export shipments primarily consisted of diplomatic moves, as diplomats rotated postings every two to four years. Although the past three years had been tough, the hard work, sacrifices, and lack of normality had been worth it. They had successfully relocated over 1,500 clients—both individuals and families—from across the globe, primarily to Hanoi and its outskirts, where large manufacturing facilities were being established. Some clients relocated to Ho Chi Minh City, which offered a closer port for their operations. Among their key achievements was managing the relocation of a global car manufacturer who were setting up a production line in Vietnam.

Kate's work frequently took her to Bangkok to meet prospective clients or attend international networking events. As was customary for anyone leaving Vietnam, she often carried a shopping list of British essentials for expatriates: pounds of Cumberland sausages, British bacon, Marmite, branded tea and coffee, and English cheddar cheese, to name a few. With her connections to the country managers of major international airlines operating in Vietnam, she always ensured she had access to dry ice boxes to safely transport these goods as carry-on luggage.

Chapter 16: Western Shadows in the East

On one particular trip in October 1997, Kate was walking along a main road in Bangkok when she spotted a large neon sign bearing the name of a well-known UK supermarket chain. She froze, thinking she must be hallucinating. This was a former client of hers in the UK, who had once assured her that if they ever expanded into Asia, they would contact her to handle the relocation.

Her initial reaction was one of disappointment—they hadn't reached out and had seemingly chosen a competitor. Determined to understand why, Kate decided to call her UK contact, Edith, to investigate.

After waiting a couple of hours for the time difference, Kate made the call.

'Hi, Edith, it's Kate. Yes, I know it's been a very long time—glad you're still there. How are you?' she said, forcing herself to sound cheerful while suppressing her irritation. 'I was phoning to ask how the moves went for your team in Bangkok. When did they relocate? I haven't received any enquiries from you for quotes to support their moves,' she added lightly, masking her annoyance.

Edith sounded perplexed. 'Kate, we haven't even set up a supermarket out there, let alone relocated any management staff. I can assure you we would have contacted you if we had.'

Kate frowned. 'Well, there's a store here with identical signage, layout, item labelling and even plastic bags. It's unmistakably your branding. I'll take some photos and email them to you.'

'Please do, Kate. I'll escalate this to the directors immediately. Don't be surprised if I call you back later and ask you to meet them at the airport. Honestly, Kate, we haven't set up an operation there, but it sounds like that might change very soon! Thank you for calling—I really appreciate it,' Edith said, her tone now urgent.

Kate hung up, feeling both vindication and anticipation. Whatever was happening, she was determined to ensure her company remained in the running for future opportunities.

Oh God, Kate thought. *I've opened up a can of worms here.* Her curiosity got the better of her, and she stepped inside the supermarket to investigate further. The layout was strikingly similar to that of its UK counterpart, with identical product labelling and branding. *How on earth did they manage this?* Kate wondered. The packaging was almost indistinguishable from the UK, and she couldn't fathom how they'd even replicated the taste. Thailand was well-known for producing counterfeit goods—handbags, shoes, clothing, electronics—but food items were a surprise.

A few hours later, her phone rang. It was Edith.

'Hi, Kate. Right, I've had an emergency meeting with the board of directors, and it's been agreed that two of them will fly out on the overnight flight tonight! Can I ask a favour— would you meet them at the airport and take them to this so-called supermarket? Of course, we'll compensate you for your time,' Edith said in a rush, barely pausing for breath.

'No problem, Edith. I'm happy to help. But you can return the favour by awarding me the relocation contract when you start moving your managers and team out here. Send me the flight details and names, and I'll meet them at the airport. I'll arrange to borrow a car from our Bangkok office. Which hotel will they be staying at?' Kate replied, unable to resist smiling to herself.

'Deal. I will share their flight details with you,' Edith said decisively before hanging up.

The following morning, Kate met the two directors at the airport. She took them to their hotel so they could drop off their luggage, freshen up and change into casual clothing—something Kate suggested so they wouldn't stand out. She handed them some Thai baht and drove them to the supermarket in question.

The look of utter shock and horror on their faces as they surveyed the store said it all. They discreetly took hundreds of photos, capturing the layout, products, marketing materials, uniforms, tills and signage. They even purchased several items—mostly non-perishables—to bring back to the UK for analysis, along with a few perishables they tasted back at the hotel. Kate, meanwhile, waited in the car further up the road, preferring to stay out of the immediate storm she sensed was brewing.

That evening, over dinner, the directors bombarded her with questions. She answered as best she could, sensing that this incident would trigger swift and decisive action.

By mid-1998, a fully-fledged supermarket of the said brand had opened in Bangkok. Kate and Stuart coordinated the relocations from the UK via their Bangkok office, handling the moves for expatriate managers, buyers, project managers and technical teams. Kate knew this was just the beginning; she foresaw a surge of activity as the company expanded further into Thailand.

Kate and Stuart were sitting on their balcony overlooking Westlake, watching the fishermen at work and reflecting on the three years they had spent in Hanoi. Simply being there, surviving the challenges and building a thriving business felt like an achievement in itself, Kate thought. They had also made lifelong friends, many from Australia, Canada, New Zealand and the UK, whose company they treasured.

Hanoi had undergone rapid change and development during their time there. New buildings, hotels and international schools had sprung up, alongside substantial improvements to infrastructure. However, Kate felt some sadness as she observed the creeping influence of Western culture. She recalled supporting relocations for major companies that had contributed to these changes and so-called improvements, and she felt conflicted.

She vividly remembered sharing drinks with the country managers of two major brands—one producing fizzy drinks, the other toothpaste. She had quipped, 'I wouldn't be surprised if there's a collaboration at Head Office. One product decaying teeth and the other trying to clean and protect them.' The joke hadn't gone down well.

Kate often wrestled with the ethical implications of their work. They were moving expatriates, building materials, factory equipment, steel and prefabricated structures for manufacturing plants and hotels. One hotel had even shipped over prefabricated block sections that were slotted together on-site. *It's such a simplified approach to building,* she mused.

Western influence was becoming more apparent in the younger Vietnamese generation. Many aspired to Western fashion and ideals. While books and newspapers were still scarce, Vietnamese airline crew often collected discarded international newspapers from flights. At home, their families would carefully iron out the creases and resell the newspapers to expatriates and curious locals eager to glimpse the outside world.

Kate had arranged with a few airline crew members to supply her with newspapers regularly. She paid them the going rate, which served a dual purpose. Not only did the papers keep her informed about global events—helping her identify potential business opportunities—but she also used them as teaching materials for her English classes.

The classes were still a keystone of her weekly routine and had grown notably over the past three years. Kate was delighted to see the mutual respect and amity develop between the men and women in the group. She had taught them how to collaborate on presentations, debate topics in English, and engage in structured discussions. Watching their progress was both fascinating and exhilarating.

Though her Vietnamese was still a work in progress, Kate could now manage daily conversations and navigate her work with increasing confidence.

Her 'best friend,' the motorbike lady, had been a constant source of support and fun. They had formed a mutually beneficial partnership: the motorbike lady taught Kate Vietnamese while Kate helped her improve her English. They had developed a close working relationship, and Kate appreciated the time they spent together.

When Kate travelled to Ho Chi Minh City for her biweekly visits, it gave her friend the chance to take on other jobs. The arrangement worked well for both of them, and Kate cherished the connections she had built in Vietnam—both professional and personal.

Kate had been taken aback by the stark differences between Hanoi and Ho Chi Minh City (HCMC) during her first few visits. HCMC seemed at least fifteen years ahead of Hanoi in almost every respect—roads, infrastructure, buildings, businesses and the sheer number of Westerners settling there. The pace of growth in HCMC across all sectors was astonishing, yet it left Kate with mixed emotions.

While progress could be wonderful, it saddened her to see so many Vietnamese traditions and cultural nuances eroding in the south. HCMC seemed to have lost part of its soul and identity in the race for modernisation. The southern Vietnamese appeared less patient, eager for Western products and lifestyles, and perpetually rushed to complete tasks or move from one place to another. Compared to the North, the South felt less safe and trustworthy to Kate. She encountered more underhanded dealings, which she neither engaged in nor condoned, unlike some of her new competitors in the industry.

The roads were a chaotic tangle of vehicles, and Kate never felt at ease in the taxis she had to rely on. Unlike in Hanoi, where she was comfortable zipping around on motorbikes, the thought of riding one in HCMC didn't even cross her mind.

Chapter 17: A Ball to Remember

Over the past three years, Kate had travelled to HCMC every fortnight, staying for two weeks each time. Her trips were strictly business-focused, filled with client appointments during the day and networking events in the evenings whenever possible. She stayed in the same hotel each visit, and while the familiarity was comforting, she was still shadowed everywhere she went. Her faxes and phone calls continued to be monitored, a continual reminder of the watchful environment she worked within.

The hardest part of these trips, however, was being away from Stuart. It was made worse by the relentless questions she faced during her evening engagements.

'You're married? Where is your husband?' was a question she was asked at nearly every event. After nearly a year of this, some of her acquaintances—both men and women—had begun openly speculating whether Stuart even existed. The insinuations wore her down, leaving her feeling increasingly isolated.

One month back in Hanoi, Kate finally decided she had to do something.

'Please, Stuart, just this once,' she implored him. 'There's a Ball at a newly built hotel in HCMC next month. I'm so tired of the persistent questioning and the doubt that you even exist. It's not a nice experience to go through every month.' She fought back tears as she spoke.

To her relief and delight, Stuart agreed. He promised to fly down the morning of the Ball, spend the day at the office, and they would return to Hanoi together on a Saturday. Kate felt a wave of happiness and immense relief wash over her.

Excited by the prospect, Kate visited her trusted dressmaker to commission a gown for the occasion.

The idea of a ball gown brought back vivid memories of the first and only time she'd ever worn one. It had been for the International Chef's Awards at the Waldorf in London, back when she was a trainee hotel manager. She had found a beautiful dress—a black lace off-the-shoulder design, long and floaty, exuding femininity, despite her usual preference for jeans. The gown had cost her £82, an extravagant sum given that she earned only £39 a week at the time. Paying it off had taken months.

Kate had invited her father to the event, and he had been in his element, thoroughly enjoying the evening. She smiled at the memory of him sitting next to a vicar and eating the carnations from the table decorations. His antics had kept the entire table in fits of laughter all night.

Shaking herself from her reverie, Kate refocused on the task at hand. She envisioned a truly elegant dress for the upcoming Ball—sleeveless, close-fitting and trailing gracefully to the floor. She imagined it in navy silk or lace, with a discreet hook to lift the train so she could dance with Stuart. She crossed her fingers at the thought. *He's not a dancer, but there's always hope,* she mused with a smile.

Mrs Wang, her dressmaker, took precise measurements in her usual manner, helping Kate select the perfect fabric and discussing the details of the design. The anticipation of the Ball and Stuart's presence buoyed Kate's spirits as she prepared for what she hoped would be a night to remember.

A few days later, Kate was not disappointed. The dress was truly stunning—beyond anything she had imagined. With narrow straps delicately resting on her shoulders and a low back that hugged the base of her spine, it exuded sophistication. The trail was sufficiently long, and the ingenious hook at her waist allowed her to lift and secure it if she wanted to walk or dance freely.

Her only concern was that the dress's design made it impossible to wear a bra. Sensing her hesitation, the young seamstresses exchanged knowing smiles and brought out a roll of wide grey sticky tape. Laughing, they demonstrated how to use the tape to provide support in place of a bra.

'Ouch!' Kate exclaimed, wincing at the thought of removing it later. But she realised it was her only option.

The Ball was a huge success, and Kate thoroughly enjoyed herself. For the first time, she felt a sense of acceptance within HCMC's business and social circles, finally able to dispel the mystery surrounding her husband, Stuart. Many people complimented her dress, and even Stuart, who wasn't typically one for such comments, acknowledged how good she looked.

The positive experience gave Kate an idea for raising much-needed funds for the orphanage in Hanoi.

During their first two years in Vietnam, Kate had come up with the concept of holding a furniture auction at the company's old warehouse. She had reached out to all the embassies, as well as the American representative office in Hanoi, which had the largest number of stored items. With the support of a representative from an international bank, Kate arranged for a note-checking machine to verify US dollars, as counterfeit notes were rife in Vietnam at the time.

Kate catalogued over 1,500 items, noting their origin and expected value. With help from her dedicated team and a few expatriate friends, she organised the warehouse, labelling each item with its anticipated price in both US dollars and Vietnamese dong. She designed a flyer and ensured its distribution throughout businesses, expatriate groups, and local communities in Hanoi, inviting both Westerners and Vietnamese to attend the auction or view the items beforehand. She also informed local police and government officials, extending an invitation to ensure the event ran smoothly. For added security, she asked Stuart to arrange minders to oversee both the preview days and the auction itself.

On the day of the auction, Kate was prepared for a marathon effort. Wearing a bright orange outfit to stand out from the crowd, clean trainers for climbing on furniture to gain height, and a whistle hanging around her neck, she was ready to face the chaos. Despite including clear instructions in Vietnamese on the flyers, the auction began with a frenzy that bordered on a stampede.

Spotting one of her English lesson students, a policeman, in the crowd, Kate beckoned him to join her. Gratefully, he stepped up onto a table and shouted the rules to the audience in a polite but authoritative manner. Bidders were instructed to raise their numbered slips to indicate their bids. If successful, their slips would be marked with the item number and winning bid, allowing them to pay and collect their items later.

Thanks to his intervention, the event regained order. Kate had to use her whistle more times than she cared to admit, but by the end of the day, every single item was sold and removed from the warehouse.

The cashier encountered around 30% counterfeit US dollar notes, but those attempting to pay with fake currency were either sent away to retrieve legal tender or lost their bids, with the items re-entered into the auction.

The auction was an undeniable success. Kate was exhausted, her voice hoarse from hours of shouting over the crowd, but she was elated by the outcome. It had taken five intense days of preparation and execution, but the results were worth it.

The embassies, thrilled with the proceeds and the elimination of their monthly storage bills, expressed their gratitude and even insisted on contributing to Kate and Stuart's efforts. While Kate initially declined, she eventually agreed on the condition that the funds go toward paying the local staff and purchasing clothes, bedding and supplies for the orphanage.

Kate had learned an important lesson early on: during their first fundraising effort, cash donations to local authorities had not been used for the orphanage. From then on, she ensured funds were spent directly on purchasing necessary items or sourcing donations of materials and supplies. This approach worked brilliantly, and the visible improvements in the children's lives brought joy to everyone involved.

The collaboration among the international women in Hanoi, primarily the wives of both diplomatic and non-diplomatic expatriates, was particularly rewarding. For many, it provided a sense of purpose and accomplishment while creating a tight-knit, supportive community.

Encouraged by the success, many embassies suggested Kate replicate the auction in HCMC, where consulates also had excess furniture in scattered storage locations. She eagerly began planning an identical event, notifying officials and generating significant interest during the preview days.

However, on the morning of the auction, the officials abruptly rescinded their approval, cancelling the event without explanation. Despite Kate and her team's best efforts to inform attendees, many still turned up. She managed to collect their contact details and offered private viewings to sell the items discreetly. Though far less efficient, she was determined to fulfil her promise to the consulates and free up space for her planned document storage facility in HCMC.

Kate and Stuart had formed a small but close-knit group of friends with whom they shared unforgettable mountain biking adventures. The group, while male-dominated, warmly embraced Kate, Rosie, and Anne as equals. Kate chuckled to herself, thinking, *Good thing they were supportive. If not, I would've had a few choice words to say about it!*

They had come to an agreement with one of the lorry drivers to transport all the mountain bikes to their chosen destinations. The group collectively contributed to the cost, which made the arrangement both practical and affordable. Planning these outings took considerable effort. Routes were carefully researched to ensure safety—both in terms of terrain and local security—and to match the group's varying levels of skill. Scenic beauty was also a priority, as the rides offered a chance to escape the hustle and bustle of their daily lives and immerse themselves in Vietnam's stunning countryside.

Everyone agreed that these excursions were both liberating and restorative. They loved the fresh air, the physical exercise and the opportunity to interact with local villagers along the way. For Kate, however, the rides came with one frustration: her inability to take photos while navigating the challenging terrain. The narrow dirt tracks, steep hills, valleys, rivers, and muddy stretches demanded her full attention. Still, these trips were a wonderful way to recharge and regain balance amidst the pressures of life.

The rides weren't without their challenges, some of which were downright terrifying. Difficult terrain was a given, but there were also occasional encounters with the military or police in certain districts. They often had to explain they were cycling purely for pleasure and not looking for anything suspicious.

On one memorable ride, the group found themselves in a picturesque area that Kate imagined would transform into a fast-flowing river during the wet season. At that moment, however, it was dry as a bone. Suddenly, half a dozen armed soldiers appeared, rifles pointed directly at them. They had emerged from nowhere, leaving the entire group frozen in fear. Ken, along with another friend, managed to communicate with the lead officer, reassuring him that they were simply enjoying the countryside. The soldiers eventually instructed them to turn back, barring them from cycling further.

Later, Ken investigated and discovered that the area they had been heading towards an area that housed a large satellite receiving dish and other sensitive communications equipment critical to the government's military and national security.

Chapter 18: The Billabong Bar and Christmas

*A*fter intense weeks of work, Friday evenings at the Billabong Bar were a much-needed reprieve. Run by members of the Australian Embassy's civilian staff, the compact bar was a hub of warmth, laughter and friendship. Kate and Stuart formed some lifelong friendships there, and although many of these friends had since either returned to Australia or moved to other countries around the world, Kate still kept in touch with several of them. Whenever she could, she arranged to meet up, though such occasions were rare.

It was at the Billabong Bar that Kate learned to play darts. Though not particularly competitive, she enjoyed the social banter and the relaxed atmosphere.

Something that never ceased to amaze Kate was the way Vietnamese people—men, women, and even children—could crouch effortlessly for long periods. Whether at markets, beer stalls, food vendors, or playing cards by the lakes, they balanced perfectly with their knees bent, feet flat on the ground, and upper legs resting against their calves, all without their bottoms touching the ground or toppling over.

Kate had tried countless times to replicate this position but never managed it. Even practising Tai Chi on the bridge over the river in Hanoi several mornings a week didn't help her master the skill. A woman from her English class had invited her to join these sessions, and Kate found them both liberating and meditative. The deliberate, slow movements required her to focus on her breathing, posture, and balance, offering a calming start to the day. It reminded her of her gymnastics training at school, rekindling her body's sense of alignment and control.

Miss Hoa had settled into a comfortable routine with Kate and Stuart, and they got along well. Miss Hoa especially loved when they hosted friends, networking events, or post-Hash gatherings at their home. Every empty beer could earn her 200 dong at the local recycling centre, and she enthusiastically collected them.

One day, while helping Miss Hoa clean the downstairs floors, Kate decided to stand on a large wet towel and 'mop' the floors by sliding around as though she were dancing. Miss Hoa had watched, bewildered, before bursting into laughter, clearly thinking Kate had lost her mind.

Recently, though, Miss Hoa had faced a deeply sorrowful time. She had become pregnant but was not allowed to keep the child, as during this time, Vietnamese law prohibited women from having another baby until their first child was at least five years old. Her daughter was only 18 months old. Kate, with the help of Hun's translation, tried to comfort Miss Hoa and assure her of her support, but she knew there was little she could do to ease such pain.

One early Christmas in Hanoi, Kate had made a list of seventeen potential presents for Stuart—everything from mountain bike accessories to cufflinks (though she couldn't quite recall why she'd included those). On a rare business trip to Singapore, she had scoured shops for gifts but came up empty-handed.

In the end, she bought Stuart a watch he had wanted for years. She had planned to keep it as a surprise for his birthday, but the watch's persistent beeping in the cupboard gave it away, and she ended up giving it to him early. Stuart had been deeply touched by the effort Kate had gone to.

Navigating Hanoi's expatriate circles could often be challenging. While Kate and Stuart moved seamlessly between various social and professional groups, occasional tensions arose when their friends from different circles clashed. One Christmas, they had arranged lunch with their mountain biking friends, only to discover that another group had invited themselves to join—without informing them until the day itself. Knowing some personalities didn't mix well, Kate and Stuart tactfully spoke to the hotel team to ensure the seating was set to avoid conflict.

That Christmas, Kate had longed for roast potatoes, which sadly did not appear, but the day ended on a joyful note when they and their friends decided to treat their Cyclo drivers to a ride in their own seats. The men pedalled the drivers around Hanoi, laughing uproariously. Ever the adventurer, Kate decided to try cycling a cyclo herself. The bikes had no handlebar brakes, and she could barely reach the pedals while seated on the high saddle. Climbing onto it was an ordeal in itself, but the challenge caused endless laughter among the group.

On Boxing Day, Kate and Stuart once again hosted the Christmas Hash, with around forty people turning up to take part. To ensure it remained a relaxed affair, it was clearly designated as a Walking Hash—Kate's excuse being that everyone's stomachs would still be too full from the indulgences of Christmas Day.

Kate prepared a comforting pumpkin soup for after the walk, served with a rare treat of cheddar cheese and plenty of *bánh mì*. They had also managed to procure a few boxes of red wine, enough to make mulled wine for everyone as they arrived back from the Hash. The warm, spiced drink was a hit, especially in the cooler December air.

The event was a resounding success. Over the following days, many attendees sent Kate and Stuart thoughtful messages, cards, and even small gifts, expressing their gratitude. Several remarked that the Hash had truly lifted their spirits, helping to combat homesickness and the sadness of missing family at such a poignant time of year.

That New Year's Eve, the Australian Billabong Bar opened its doors for an informal celebration. Guests brought along crates of beer and any wine they had acquired in previous months. Kate and Stuart knew about 80% of the people there, and the evening turned into a lively, enjoyable gathering.

Still, as much as Kate relished these moments, she couldn't help but miss the New Year's Eve traditions she had left behind. She longed for the celebrations with family and friends back home, as well as her personal tradition of finding a quiet spot by the sea to reflect and write down her dreams for the year ahead. It had been three years since she had last done so, which was sad in itself as Kate had made this a tradition of hers since her late teens.

'Maybe I could take myself off to a boat on Hoàn Kiếm Lake one day soon and just sit there,' she mused wistfully. But she shook her head with a wry smile. 'Get real, Kate,' she muttered to herself.

By late 1997, Kate had started to feel more at ease in Ho Chi Minh City. She had managed to make a few friends she could call on during her visits, which meant her evenings weren't solely about networking or entertaining clients.

However, there was an increasing sense of unrest within Vietnam during that time. The country felt torn between embracing progress and maintaining strict governmental control. While the government pursued development, they were reluctant to loosen the constraints progress often demanded.

One significant change was the imposition of steep taxes on joint ventures and foreign companies operating in Vietnam, requiring them to pay almost 90% of their profits to the government. Additionally, the government restricted international companies from transferring money out of Vietnam to pay overseas suppliers. Payments could only be made through domestic banks. These policies left many corporations questioning whether operating in Vietnam was worth the effort due to financial constraints and if it was financially viable to continue.

Despite the challenges, Kate and Stuart continued to enjoy their mountain biking expeditions. Their group of friends, a mix of men and women, seemed to flourish with each ride, their confidence growing visibly. The routes often led them over rough terrain, steep mountain climbs and precarious descents, but the camaraderie and the stunning scenery made it worthwhile.

The group had affectionately named themselves the 'Throbbers,' a nod to the inevitable soreness in their arms, legs and bums after every ride.

Unfortunately, not every expedition went smoothly. On one occasion, after a particularly gruelling climb and a steep descent, one of their friends lost control and went headfirst over his handlebars. His helmet was shattered, and he suffered deep cuts requiring stitches. It was a harrowing experience.

An hour-long drive back to Hanoi and a long wait at the hospital followed before an expatriate doctor could treat him. Though badly shaken, their friend was remarkably resilient—just three weeks later, he was back on his bike, ready to join the group for another adventure.

The airport road had recently been much improved with actual tarmac being laid, and a central reservation was installed along its length in an attempt to manage the ever-increasing volume of cars, lorries and motorbikes. However, this modernization had left many of the local farmers and their livestock utterly bewildered. Buffalo, ducks and other animals could no longer be herded freely across the road from field to field, much to the frustration of their owners.

Kate and her motorbike lady 'best friend' had recently experienced the perils of navigating the chaotic traffic on Hanoi's roads. While riding together, they found themselves squeezed between two lorries, battling for dominance on the narrow road. No matter how skillfully her 'friend' steered the motorbike, the trucks refused to yield, leaving them with no choice but to veer off the road. They collided heavily with a concrete wall—certainly a better outcome than being crushed beneath a lorry, but still a terrifying ordeal.

Shaken and bruised, they called Mr Houng, who promptly arrived to take them to the hospital in Hanoi.

Upon arrival, Kate was ushered into a room that looked more like a shed than a medical facility. The X-ray machine appeared to be a prototype from decades past, and the room itself was far from sterile. As she sat waiting, two rats scurried across the floor, their presence so casual it was as if they belonged there. Mosquitoes buzzed incessantly, adding to the discomfort of the already unnerving environment.

Till now, Kate had grown somewhat accustomed to the presence of rats. During heavy rains, the dirt track leading to their house would often flood up to their calves. Kate had taken to wearing plastic sandals for the walk home, but even these couldn't prepare her for the first time she felt something alive skittering across her feet. She had screamed, frozen in horror at the sensation of something wriggling against her skin. Her first thought was that it was a snake slithering over her toes. When she realized it was a rat, she felt a surprising sense of relief—until she saw the size of it. Some of the rats were enormous, easily as big as rabbits.

Back in the x-ray room, the ordeal took another strange turn. The doctors insisted that Kate remove her blouse and bra to allow them to x-ray her left arm. Sensing something off, Kate flatly refused. Instead, she demanded a pair of scissors and instructed them to cut the sleeve off her blouse, exposing only the injured arm. Later, she learned the unsettling reason behind their insistence. It wasn't uncommon for Western women to be asked to remove their tops unnecessarily during X-rays. The resulting images would sometimes be sold to interested parties, a deeply invasive and exploitative practice. True to form, Kate stood her ground and ensured her dignity remained intact.

The X-ray revealed two fractures in the humerus just above her elbow in her left arm. The hospital provided her with a sling, and she immediately went to check on her motorbike friend, who thankfully had no serious injuries. Outside, Mr Houng waited patiently, with the battered motorbike half hanging out of the boot of his car.

Returning home, Kate found herself frustrated by her newfound limitations. Being left-handed, she struggled to adapt to using her right hand for everything. Typing emails one-handed became her new normal, and while she could technically write with her right hand, it was little more than an illegible scrawl.

Her predicament also brought some unexpected moments of levity. Vietnamese people often smiled broadly or giggled when they saw her writing with her left hand. Hun once told her that writing left-handed was seen as a sign of intelligence in Vietnamese culture. Kate, ever practical, brushed off the compliments with a smile, but the sentiment stayed with her as a small silver lining during her recovery.

In the days following, Kate and Stuart had experienced a particularly unsettling ordeal with a termite infestation in their home. With the help of Hun, their ever-faithful interpreter, they explained to their landlord that they could hear an incessant tapping sound emanating from the wooden window frames, internal doors, and skirting boards throughout the property. The noise grew louder with each passing day, leaving them convinced that the wood was teeming with hatching termites eating their way through the wood. Despite their protests and warnings, the situation escalated due to inaction by their landlord.

One evening, after returning from the office, they were greeted by a nightmarish scene: the entire ground floor was swarming with thousands of flying termites. The sheer number of termites was overwhelming, and the sight was nothing short of horrifying. Desperate, they used all four cans of fly spray they had in the house, filling the air with a pungent, sickly smell, causing both of them to cough profusely and be unable to breathe normally as the termites were falling onto them and the surrounding surfaces. The floor was soon littered with dead termites, and Kate had to steady herself to avoid being sick at the grotesque scene. They spent the whole evening sweeping and hoovering up the termites.

Upon seeking advice, someone recommended a pest control company called Pest Busters, run by a Singaporean woman and a Vietnamese gentleman. With little to lose, they contacted the company and were reassured that this was a common issue in the region. Unknowingly, Kate and Stuart had actually done their job for them the night before by 'terminating' the termites. Miss Hoa had asked Hun to interpret the Pest Busters's statement to them after they had visited the house. In theory, all of the termites had hatched, exposed themselves in the house and the fly spray had hopefully killed all of them. Unless Kate and Stuart heard any further noises in the wood, there was nothing else they could do.

Chapter 19: A Coastal Reprieve

By February 1998, four years into their time in Vietnam, Kate and Stuart were ready for a much-needed escape. Their short break in Nha Trang was set to be something special. As usual, Kate had spent two weeks in Ho Chi Minh City, and Stuart had joined her for a couple of days before they flew to the coastal town. The flight, lasting about an hour, was an adventure in itself. The plane, which Kate likened to something out of the Dark Ages, was a small biplane. To her amazement, the pilot had to manually spin the propeller to start the engine. There were only six passengers on the flight, including them.

The airport in Nha Trang was reminiscent of their first arrival in Hanoi: a simple affair. They disembarked onto the tarmac and walked across the runway to a warehouse-like building that served as the terminal. There was no luggage carousel; there were just three Vietnamese women dressed in traditional áo dài, along with several armed policemen who observed them as they passed through with their hand luggage.

The hotel had arranged for a minibus to collect them and the other passengers. The drive to the resort was idyllic, passing through small villages where hay was laid out on dirt tracks to dry in preparation for winter. Hens and ducks roamed freely, and Kate noticed sweetcorn kernels spread across the rooftops of bamboo huts, drying under the sun. She presumed this was winter fodder for cattle. The rustic scenery transported her back to Hanoi in 1994, evoking a sense of nostalgia.

The other passengers introduced themselves during the drive. Jim and his partner Louise were also staying at the hotel, while the remaining two passengers were simply catching a lift, as there were no taxis available at the airport.

Nha Trang, situated on Vietnam's south-central coast, was a stunning coastal resort with pristine beaches, crystal-clear waters teeming with coral and marine life, and a rich history of temples and pagodas. At the time, the only visible Western influence was the newly built hotel where Kate and Stuart were staying. The modern establishment, with its luxurious amenities, was in stark contrast to the traditional surroundings. Kate had learned of the hotel's opening through her work, as the General Manager, Ross, had been relocated from Australia to oversee operations. She was relieved to hear that his shipping container, carrying all his household and personal belongings, had cleared customs without a hitch. The team in Ho Chi Minh City had ensured the delivery went smoothly, earning Ross's high praise.

As they arrived at the hotel, Kate was immediately struck by the grandeur of the entrance. The path was flanked by palm trees and adorned with small Buddha statues interspersed with enormous terracotta pots brimming with vibrant tropical plants. Two large tiger statues stood guard at the entrance, adding to the sense of grandeur. Inside, the reception area was breathtaking. The marble floors gleamed, and the air of opulence was palpable. The oak reception desk faced a panoramic view of the ocean framed by swaying palm trees. The salty sea breeze wafted through, instantly soothing Kate's senses.

Ross greeted them warmly with champagne and canapés, joining them and the other six guests before they were shown to their rooms. The hotel was still in its pre-opening phase, and this visit was part of a 'test run' organised by Ross to assess operations and provide on-the-job training for the staff. Kate and Stuart, along with a select group of invitees, were happy to participate.

Kate felt right at home in the hotel's luxurious setting. Even if there were minor mishaps during the trial run, she didn't mind at all. As she put it, 'Better now than during the official opening.' Her background in hotel management surfaced as she observed the operations with a critical but empathetic eye.

Her thoughts drifted back to her previous career, where one of the hotels she had managed was previously a stately home transformed into a four-star country house hotel near London. She recalled an innovative training weekend she had organised for her team, where all of the staff swapped their chosen professions for the roles of other colleagues to foster respect and collaboration between all the departments. She had offered forty clients to stay for a 'free' weekend break with their partners and advised them of the brief and purpose of the weekend and to be ready for chaos during this training.

The chaotic but insightful experience left a lasting impact on the team and brought them closer together. Reflecting on that time, she smiled, grateful for the lessons it had taught her.

Back in the present, Kate revelled in the luxury of her surroundings. The super king-size bed with its crisp cotton sheets, the opulent gold-plated taps, the enormous bath, and the private jacuzzi on the patio overlooking the ocean all felt like heaven. She sighed contentedly, feeling a rare sense of freedom.

Dinner that evening was a culinary triumph. The seafood rivalled that of the finest restaurants in London. The king prawns melted in her mouth, the lobster was the best she had ever tasted, and the imported steak was perfectly cooked—tender and succulent.

Another blessing was that neither she nor Stuart was being followed around the clock, a constant reality that had not eased during their three years of living there. She sighed again with relief as she realised their phones were no longer incessantly ringing – all calls had been redirected to the Hanoi office for three days. Only in the case of an absolute emergency would anyone be permitted to contact the hotel directly. Kate had advised the team to embrace this opportunity to shine, encouraging them to demonstrate their true abilities and qualities to Stuart during these three uninterrupted days.

As she lay in bed that night, lulled by the sound of the waves and the cool sea breeze, Kate felt an overwhelming sense of gratitude. Life in Vietnam had its trials, but moments like these made it all worthwhile.

The following day, they indulged in fresh tropical fruit and other delicacies for breakfast while gazing out over the crystal-clear ocean. The tranquillity of the morning set the tone for their day, which was spent scuba diving under the guidance of Eifion, a Welshman leading the crew. Eifion (pronounced Ivion) had established his business there after marrying a Vietnamese woman several years ago. He had previously worked as an instructor in Phuket, having left the UK in the early 1990s to pursue his love for diving and adventure.

Although both Kate and Stuart were a little out of practice, they took their time and were grateful they didn't need to dive too deep to witness the stunning coral reefs and vibrant marine life. The underwater world felt like an entirely different realm, bursting with colours and teeming with movement.

The next two days were blissfully unhurried. Mornings were spent lazing around, afternoons filled with more diving and leisurely swims, and evenings dedicated to sumptuous dinners shared with delightful company. They rounded off each night with a selection of liqueurs and speciality cocktails before retiring, content and serene.

When the time came to leave, it was a wrench to tear themselves away. They had promised to return as soon as possible and vowed to recommend the place to as many expatriates as they could. Kate had even agreed with Ross that she would write an article about the hotel in their next newsletter, which delighted him immensely.

Later that week, Sophie shared some unexpected news: Tom had been given a new posting, and they were set to move to Manila within the month. Sophie and Tom had asked Kate and Stuart to handle their packing and destination services for the move. Kate was genuinely gutted by the announcement. Sophie and her family had become a cornerstone of her life, and the thought of losing their close friendship left Kate feeling bereft. Yet, deep down, she was certain their friendship was built to last. This certainly wasn't the end.

Chapter 20: Drifting into Doubt

For the past six months, Kate had felt a growing distance between herself and Stuart. She couldn't quite put her finger on what was wrong, but something felt undeniably off. At home, he was withdrawn, barely speaking to her, let alone opening up about what might be troubling him. He had started going out alone in the evenings much more frequently, which was completely unlike him. On several occasions, he had suggested that perhaps they shouldn't work together anymore, even hinting that Kate should consider finding a different job. She hadn't taken his comments seriously, assuming it was just one of his moods. While she didn't entirely dismiss his remarks, she chose not to press the issue, though it did annoy her that he seemed to treat the matter so lightly without a proper discussion. There was no denying it—something else was going on, and Kate was determined to find out what.

One evening, Stuart came home late and announced he would be travelling to Bangkok for a meeting and would be away for a week. Kate acted as though nothing was amiss, though she couldn't shake the uneasy feeling she got from the slight edge in his voice. The following morning, he left early, apologizing for waking her but neglecting to say goodbye or even give her a kiss. During the night, Kate had scribbled a list of meats and other Western products they needed and left it on the table by the front door, having been unable to sleep. She noticed he had taken it, but her heart felt heavy, her mind swirling with unanswered questions. *What on earth was going on?* she wondered, trying to piece things together. Had she done something wrong? Was it her fault that Stuart seemed so restless and distant?

Kate pushed the troubling thoughts aside and got ready for work. She was determined to focus on the Document Storage Business Division she had been setting up in Hanoi. It was a project she'd been working on for months, with plans to expand to Ho Chi Minh City. Many of her clients had offices overflowing with paperwork, much of which needed to be kept for a minimum of seven to ten years due to Vietnamese legal requirements. Kate had secured funding through the Hanoi business and had commissioned a local factory to produce the racking for document storage. Explaining her needs to the factory was challenging, but after months of back-and-forth communication and translations, the prototype was finally completed.

The project was a triumph. She had also managed to source staple-free, foldable storage boxes during a trip to Bangkok, and after much effort, a local supplier had successfully replicated them. Kate was thrilled when the system was finally operational, and clients began signing up quickly, eager to have their documents boxed, labelled and securely stored. Within two months, all the initial racking was filled, and Kate was overjoyed. Her grandmother's motto, *'Never say never,'* echoed in her mind as she reflected on her success.

On Valentine's Day in 1998, Kate and Stuart had agreed to host the Hash. Kate had arranged for roses to be handed out to all the women as a nod to the occasion. However, Stuart had made it clear he would be going out that evening with his 'single' friends after the dinner. Kate's mind raced. *Going out with single friends on Valentine's Day? Really?* He returned in the early hours in a dreadful state.

The next morning, Kate rearranged her appointments. She knew Stuart would be nursing a hangover and wouldn't be in the office early. They needed to talk—things couldn't continue like this. When he eventually came downstairs, he made it clear he didn't want to talk. Despite her calm and gentle approach, Stuart remained closed off.

Over the following weeks, Kate tried to carry on as best she could, offering support and attempting to engage with Stuart whenever possible. But he withdrew even further. At social events, he ignored her, made a point of sitting apart from her and avoided her entirely. She later learned from other expatriates that Stuart had been going clubbing and had been seen dancing provocatively with another expatriate woman. The gossip stung.

Kate knew who the woman was—an outgoing, flirtatious figure who often commanded the attention of men at networking events. While Kate preferred a more subtle approach to socialising, this woman thrived on being the centre of attention. It broke Kate's heart to see Stuart acting like a lovestruck fool around her, though she couldn't help but feel pity for him. Deep down, she still loved him and desperately wanted to fix things. She knew the other woman was just playing with him and had no real interest, but the pain of seeing Stuart place her on a pedestal was almost too much to bear.

Was it commonplace for expatriate couples to endure such phases in their lives? Kate had seen and heard countless sorrowful stories of marriages crumbling under the strain of the expatriate lifestyle. Tales of wives silently enduring their husbands' affairs, excused under the guise of 'business trips,' were far too frequent. It was a bitter realization, but one that

Kate couldn't ignore: was this the path her own marriage was now treading?

Had Stuart's affair been born out of opportunity? Her frequent two-week stints in Ho Chi Minh City each month over the years had given him the space and freedom to meet someone else. Or, worse, did he think *she* was the one 'playing the field?' The thought sent shivers down Kate's spine. She knew herself well—she was neither the archetypal stay-at-home wife nor a dazzling beauty who turned heads in every room. But she had always been sociable, attending events with or without Stuart, enjoying her evenings responsibly and never doing anything to embarrass him.

By the end of March that year, Stuart dropped the bombshell. 'I need space,' he declared, looking at her with both guilt and detachment. 'I want to be on my own.'

Kate stared at him, her heart racing as she tried to comprehend what he was saying. 'You mean you want space to spend with *her*, don't you? Why can't you just be honest with yourself and me for once?'

'It's not like that, Kate. I just need time… to…'

'To what, Stuart? To spend more time with *her*?' Her voice cracked, the dam of her emotions finally breaking as tears streamed down her face.

'I want to live on my own. I want to be single. I've never experienced that before. I went straight from living at home to living with you. I need to know what it's like to be single.'

Kate was dumbstruck. He said it so casually, as though he were announcing a new hobby rather than shattering their lives together. She sat frozen, trembling with disbelief, her tears falling silently onto her lap.

'You were the one who wanted us to live together,' she finally whispered, her voice trembling. 'You were the one who wanted us to get married, Stuart.'

But Stuart wasn't done. 'You also need to stop working with me. Otherwise, I won't feel "single." I can't be free if we're still working in the same company. You should find a different job in Hanoi, and there are plenty of other properties you could move into.'

The words hit her like a physical blow. 'You want me to leave the job I love, the business *we* built together, the home *we* created and the friends *we* share. You're saying this is all my responsibility, while you stay exactly where you are, continuing your life as if I never existed?'

'When you are the one who wants to experience being single……surely you should be the one moving out and finding a new job, not me,' Kate said as her lips trembled with hurt and confusion.

When he slammed the door on his way out, Kate felt her world cave in. She spent the sleepless night replaying every word, every moment, trying to understand where it had all gone so wrong.

Chapter 21: Lost in Luang Prabang

Kate couldn't bring herself to admit the whole truth—not the affair, not the unravelling of her marriage—but she had to make a move. She called their company's director. She couldn't tell him the full truth—not about the affair—but she explained she had to leave. Her marriage was more important than her career, she said, even though it broke her heart. The director was kind, offering her alternative roles, but they would still require some level of interaction with Stuart, which he had explicitly forbidden.

Kate spent the next few days tying up loose ends. She packed up her belongings from the office and poured her energy into creating a comprehensive handover document for Stuart and the director. It contained every client lead, appointment, networking event and sponsorship opportunity she had meticulously built.

When Stuart walked into the office and saw her packing, his tone was sharp. 'What are you doing?'

'Isn't it obvious?' she replied without looking up, her voice thick with tears. 'I'm leaving the business, as you asked. I've prepared a full handover for you, so everything is covered.'

'You can't just leave,' he retorted condescendingly. 'You should at least work out the month. You could even work from home if you need to.'

Kate's composure finally cracked. 'You can't be serious, Stuart! After everything you've said, after *this*—how could I possibly stay and work alongside you?' She broke into uncontrollable sobs, her heartbreak spilling over.

Kate knew she couldn't stay in Hanoi. She had to get away, to clear her head. The expat community already knew about Stuart's indiscretions. The whispers and pitying looks were suffocating except for a few close friends who offered support. She couldn't keep carrying the weight of it all with dignity anymore.

She decided to go to Luang Prabang. The old royal capital of Laos had been described as Southeast Asia's last Eden, a serene escape untouched by the relentless modernisation sweeping through Vietnam. Kate needed to lose herself in a place where the line between past and present blurred, a sanctuary far removed from Hanoi's chaos or Ho Chi Minh City's aggressive modernity.

As the plane ascended, Kate stared out of the window, replaying Stuart's words in her mind. He wanted to experience being single, to live on his own, to be known as *Stuart*, not 'Kate's husband.' The sheer absurdity of it stung deeply. She closed her eyes, letting the tears fall freely. For now, she needed to be somewhere else—somewhere she could find peace amidst the ruins of her marriage.

'What? Are you leaving Hanoi? Starting a new job in another country?' Kate had asked, sobbing.

'No, I wasn't thinking of leaving my job or Vietnam,' Stuart had replied, his tone calm, almost detached.

Kate recalled the stunned horror of it all unravelling. He didn't want change—he simply didn't want *her* in his life anymore. *Why?* What had she done wrong? And why hadn't he had the courage—or even the decency or love—to sit down and talk to her about his feelings before dropping this bombshell? Her emotions were in freefall. She felt sick to her stomach, her body paralyzed yet shaking uncontrollably.

Her mind kept replaying the moment in an endless loop, each time sending her heart into a fresh wave of painful palpitations. Her eyes, swollen and raw from crying, were a physical manifestation of her inner turmoil. She no longer cared how she looked; everything she had built her life around had crumbled beneath her. Her world, her love, even her sense of self—it all felt lost.

To travel the 215 miles from Vientiane to Luang Prabang, Kate faced three options: first, up the Mekong by cargo boat— a five-to-six-day journey, provided nothing broke down and they weren't intercepted by bandits. The second option was overland via Route 13, which is notorious for its dangers and is infamous among both backpackers and expats. The third was a flight on one of Lao Aviation's ageing, creaky Russian or Chinese propeller planes.

Time was the deciding factor. Kate opted to fly, though she felt far from reassured as she boarded the rickety 17-seater plane. Peering out of the grimy window at the rugged mountains below, she reminded herself that it had been the right decision. Even when thick clouds of white vapour began pouring from the overhead compartments, condensing into droplets and soaking the startled passengers, she told herself she had made the best of the limited choices.

From above, the Laotian highlands appeared as a breathtaking, trackless expanse of lush green. Villages were scattered so sparsely that they seemed swallowed by the wilderness. Kate was in ore at how utterly untouched the land looked—no metal glinting from cars, no sign of paved roads. Homes constructed entirely of natural materials like bamboo and palm fronds were barely visible among the dense foliage.

Her thoughts turned sombre as she considered what this tranquil landscape had endured. During the 1970s, the United States relentlessly bombed Laos in a covert campaign to destroy the Ho Chi Minh Trail. More bombs had been dropped on Laos than on all of Europe during the Second World War— a relentless campaign that lasted nine years. The staggering devastation was almost unimaginable.

Yet the people had rebuilt, guided by centuries of Buddhist tradition that shaped their remarkable resilience. Their ethos of tolerance, forgiveness, and compassion was captured in the local phrase *'baw pen nyang'*—no problem, never mind, it doesn't matter. Perhaps Kate could adopt this mantra. It might help her navigate the mess of emotions swirling inside her.

Luang Prabang offered Kate an escape—a chance to breathe away from the chaos of Vietnam and the nightmare that was unfolding. Nothing, however, had prepared her for the dreamlike beauty of the place. The town lay nestled in a high valley encircled by mist-shrouded peaks. Golden temple spires emerged from dense tropical foliage, glinting in the sunlight like something out of a fairytale.

This oldest surviving Laotian town was vibrant with colours, textures and architectural styles. Ornate temples, or *wats*, with their soaring Cambodian-style eaves adorned in gilt and mosaics, stood alongside traditional teak and bamboo houses. There were pastel-coloured Vietnamese arcades, crumbling French colonial villas with half-timbered facades and walls whispering tales of history.

Kate arrived at her modest hotel mid-afternoon. Utterly drained—both emotionally and physically—she collapsed onto the bed, hugging the pillow as if it could absorb her grief. Sleep came swiftly and lasted until the next morning.

Her first day in Luang Prabang was spent wandering the streets, camera in hand. She was struck by the serenity of her surroundings—the spaciousness, the quiet, the almost sacred atmosphere. The ever-present monks, draped in their vivid orange robes, were a constant, whimsical reminder of the town's spiritual heartbeat.

Kate was particularly drawn to the monasteries, not just as historic artefacts but as vibrant, living centres of culture. Giant drums and gongs rang out like church bells, and ornately carved dragon boats were carefully tended for annual regattas. She felt her camera lens drinking in the magic, capturing great gulps of colour and life, yet somehow, the images fell short of conveying the profound peace she felt.

Meandering down a narrow, mud-paved lane, she reached the quiet banks of the Mekong River. Laundry and fishing nets hung from tree branches and bamboo racks of golden rice cakes dried in the sun. A sad-eyed boy perched listlessly on his family's boat, his gaze fixed on the water.

The word *graceful* came to mind as she framed shot after shot: the elegant sweep of temple roofs, the sleek lines of long, pencil-thin boats, the shimmering arc of a fishing net cast into the river. But no photograph could capture the true essence of the Laotian people—their gentle resilience, their quiet dignity, their unshakable peace.

Kate's heart was completely broken. What had she done wrong? Why hadn't Stuart wanted to talk it through?

She had listened to her phone messages from friends asking after her, offering help and support. Not a word from Stuart – what did that tell her?

When Kate returned to Hanoi, she found their home eerily empty. Stuart wasn't there. She placed her suitcase in the spare room, poured herself a drink, and climbed into bed, knowing full well she wouldn't sleep. She had told Stuart she was coming back that day, but his absence spoke volumes.

In the early hours of the morning, she heard the door creak open. Stuart entered the bedroom, standing in the doorway like a stranger.

'How about we have three months apart and see how it goes?' he said flatly. 'Maybe I just need to get this out of my system.'

Kate, desperate to salvage their marriage, stupidly agreed. She didn't have the strength to argue or insist that *he* should be the one to leave. Everything still felt too raw, too calculated. She realised with sinking clarity that Stuart hadn't even asked where she'd been for the past week, let alone what she planned to do next. Did he simply not care anymore?

Her rational mind was urging her to stand up and fight, to tell Stuart to pack his bags, leave their home, his job and Hanoi, and start afresh elsewhere—a new job, new country, new home and a new circle of friends. If he was so intent on experiencing the single life, he ought to fully embrace it. But the fight in her had drained away.

The hurt was even more profound because Stuart had not asked Kate where she'd been during the past week. *How could you not even leave a message just to make sure I was safe at least* – Kate had wanted to ask but did not have the courage to. Was the fact that he simply didn't care anymore the real truth?

That truth sat heavily in her chest.

She sorted out the money owed to her from the company for the month, used the return leg of her outbound ticket, and booked a flight back to the UK, with onward travel to Spain. She decided to stay in the apartment there—her sanctuary of sorts. The idea of staying in the UK was unbearable; their home was rented out, and she couldn't face the barrage of well-meaning but overwhelming questions from family and friends. Despite their good intentions, she knew she wouldn't cope and was terrified she'd just break down into endless tears.

She had already cried so much, and she hated herself for it. It was so unlike her—this panic, confusion and flood of emotion. It made her feel weak and exposed. Yet, no matter how hard she tried to hold it all in, sometimes it was as though her body took over, demanding she release the hurt and anguish. It was as if nature whispered, *'Don't suppress it. Let it out. Breathe.'*

After saying her goodbyes to her closest friends, she endured the long-haul flight to Spain via London, with several tedious stops in transit lounges along the way. She had decided not to contact her family until she had regained some sense of composure. Even her dad and stepmother didn't know she was arriving in Spain, though their home was only half an hour's drive from the apartment.

When Kate finally reached the apartment, she felt utterly spent, her heart heavy with exhaustion and sorrow. She picked up a few basic provisions after getting off the train from the airport. Unlocking the door, she pushed it open and dragged her two suitcases and a bag inside. She turned on the fridge and placed the groceries inside. The air inside was stale and musty; dust lingered on the surfaces, and cobwebs hung lazily from the ceiling and light fixtures. Pulling back the curtains, she unlatched the large bay window and inhaled deeply, letting the salty air fill her lungs.

The rhythmic sound of the waves moving gently up and down the sand with the tide seemed to synchronise with her own breathing, bringing a faint sense of calm. Exhausted, she collapsed onto the bed and slept deeply, not waking until late the following morning.

Chapter 22: At a Standstill

When she awoke, the warm, light breeze flowing through the open window reminded her of where she was. Stretching, she made herself a coffee. Still, in the same clothes she had travelled and slept in, she eased into the old rocking chair, swaying gently back and forth as her gaze wandered out of the window.

The sea stretched out before her, calm and constant, and for the first time in what felt like forever, Kate allowed herself to simply be still.

Kate spent most of the day slumped in the same spot, only getting up to make another drink or shuffle to the bathroom. For the next five days, she barely ate, spoke to no one and ignored every phone call. She shut herself away completely, cocooned in silence and isolation.

On the sixth day, a knock on the apartment door broke the oppressive stillness. She shuffled to the door and opened it to find her dad standing there. His face was pale and drawn, etched with worry.

'I'm sorry, Dad,' she mumbled, tears welling in her eyes. 'I should have let you and Mum know, but... I just couldn't talk to anyone. I just...' Her voice faltered, and the words caught in her throat as she collapsed into his arms, sobbing uncontrollably.

'It's alright, love. No need to apologise. The important thing is we know where you are, and we know you're safe.

That's all that matters,' he said softly, his voice full of a tenderness she hadn't heard from him before.

'Probably a silly question, but... have you eaten?' he asked gently.

Kate shook her head, her eyes darting around the room. The coffee mugs scattered across the surfaces, the unopened suitcases slumped in the corner, and her reflection in the dark window—dishevelled hair, blotchy face and the faint smell of unwashed clothes—made her feel small and ashamed.

'Why don't you come and stay with us for a few days?' her dad offered, his concern unmistakable. 'We won't ask any questions. I promise.'

She hesitated, her lip trembling. 'I can't, Dad. I just... I need to be here and try to...' Her words dissolved into tears again, her shoulders shaking under the weight of her emotions.

'Alright, I won't push you,' he said, his voice steady but kind. 'You know where we are. Call me anytime, and I'll come and get you, no matter what.'

'Thanks, Dad. And... thank you for looking for me,' she murmured, her voice barely audible. 'Could you just let Mum know I'm alright? Tell her I'll call her in a few days. I promise.'

They hugged tightly, an embrace that felt like a bridge across the chasm of pain she'd been living in. It was the closest she'd felt to her Dad in years, and she realised how much his care meant to her now.

The next morning, Kate finally mustered the energy to take a long, hot shower. She slowly unpacked her suitcases, folding her clothes into the freshly cleaned cupboards and wardrobe. She cleaned the apartment, scrubbing away the stale air and the shadows of her despair. Then, as promised, she gave her mum a brief call—just enough to reassure her she was okay, but nothing more. She still wasn't ready to face long conversations or probing questions. She retreated back into her fragile bubble.

Later that afternoon, another knock came at the door. She froze, knowing it could only be her dad or stepmum. But the thought of opening the door and breaking down again was unbearable. She stayed rooted in place, silent.

'There's a saucepan of homemade soup here for you, Kate,' her dad called through the door. 'Just reheat it when you're ready. It'll keep for a few days.'

'Thanks, Dad,' she whispered, her voice cracking. She heard his footsteps retreating and felt a pang of gratitude she couldn't quite articulate.

One week bled into two, then three, before Kate found the strength to properly call her mum and explain what had happened. She kept her replies to texts and emails short, letting people know she was safe but avoiding anything deeper. The idea of engaging in lengthy conversations was exhausting.

Eventually, she accepted her dad and stepmum's offer to stay with them for a few days. With a little more composure, Kate explained what had been going on, why she'd come to Spain and how she was trying to find her footing again.

She was surprised by the flood of messages she'd received—texts, emails and voicemails from people who'd heard snippets of her situation. She replied briefly, out of courtesy rather than interest. It all felt distant and unreal like it was happening to someone else.

One morning, as she stared out of the window, the endless sound of the waves in the background, she muttered to herself, 'Get a grip, Kate. Snap out of it. Carrying on like this isn't going to solve anything.'

On the Monday of the fourth week, she walked to a nearby shop, bought a pack of pens and a notebook and settled by the seafront with a coffee. She needed a plan—something to structure her days and pull herself out of this limbo.

She jotted down her thoughts:

• Join a Spanish class—there was one nearby offering two-hour lessons five days a week. Even if she didn't retain much, it would give her a focus.

• Find a job—anything to earn a bit of money and keep her afloat while she figured things out.

• Walk along the beach every day—at least three miles, to clear her mind and rebuild her strength.

• Stop expecting communication from Stuart—easier said than done. Every time she thought about him, the tears came, her heart breaking at the memory of how he'd only called once since she left. He had not returned any of her calls or replied to her emails or texts in four weeks.

The last point lingered on the page, taunting her with its uncertainty. *What if he doesn't want me back after this?* she wondered, her chest tightening. *What if three months of being single makes him realise he wants to stay that way?*

And then, *What will I do with my life if that happens?*

Too many questions for now—just go for a walk by the sea, Kate told herself.

Chapter 23: A Flicker of Hope

Over the next four days, she threw herself into pounding the esplanade, determined to find work. She went in and out of every business along the beachfront—hotels, bars, paddleboat rental units, even the local shops selling souvenirs and beach gear. She approached everyone, including the 'lookie-lookie' man who patrolled the beach selling fizzy drinks and snacks to sunbathers. But there was one major obstacle—she didn't speak Spanish. It quickly became clear that this would hinder her at every turn.

Finally, on the fourth day, she emerged from a nightclub located at the far end of the beach. It wasn't in the best location—half a mile from the bustling town centre meant it saw little natural footfall of clients entering. Nevertheless, they offered her a job promoting the club. Her role was to distribute flyers and try to draw in potential customers along the seafront. It wasn't glamorous, but it was something.

Kate had also started Spanish lessons. They gave her a reason to get up in the morning, but absorbing and remembering the information was a struggle. Still, she persevered. On top of that, she kept up her daily beach walks, covering several miles a day to clear her head and stay active.

'Just keep doing this,' she whispered to herself. 'That's all you need to do for now.' She was grateful that the apartment had no mortgage attached and it was inexpensive to run. At least food in Spain was relatively cheap at the time.

For the next two months, Kate stuck to her routine. She went to her lessons, handed out flyers and focused on small, manageable goals. Occasionally, she would meet her dad and stepmum for lunch or coffee by the seafront, or they would have her over for dinner. Though she appreciated their company immensely, she was determined to stand on her own two feet. Another reason was that she had thought the next two months would fly by, and then she and Stuart would be back together – working things out.

'Rent the apartment out, Kate,' they had suggested. 'Come and live with us. You can use the little Fiesta to get to work.'

But Kate knew she needed her own space—to think, to heal and to avoid the pressure of constantly explaining herself to family friends who wanted to know what was happening.

One morning, as she sipped her first coffee of the day, she opened her emails while gazing out at the ocean. The soft swish of the waves against the sand and the salty breeze wafting through the open window gave her a rare sense of peace. She inhaled deeply, letting herself savour the moment.

Then she saw it.

Hi Kate,

I need more time. Three months isn't long enough for me to figure out what I want. It needs to be six months.

Stuart.

Kate slumped back in her chair, gripping the armrests as her head fell backwards.

'What? How... How could he?' she mumbled. 'How could he be so hard... so cold? Not even a phone call. Just one sentence—that's all I'm worth to him?'

The email paralysed her for the entire day. She couldn't work, couldn't face people, couldn't even bring herself to eat or walk along the beach. Instead, she curled up on her bed and wept, the tears coming in relentless waves.

The following morning, her phone buzzed, jolting her awake. She had left the window open, and the cool morning air filled the room.

'Kate, are you okay? Where are you? It's noon—you were supposed to be here at 10,' Stephan's voice crackled down the line.

'Oh, God, I'm so sorry. Give me an hour—I'll make up the time, I promise,' she whispered hoarsely.

'Are you sure you're alright? You sound awful,' he replied with genuine concern.

'Yes.' Kate hung up, showered quickly and walked up to the nightclub to collect the flyers.

Stephan, the club's owner, was about her height with a solid build. His tousled blonde hair hung loosely to his shoulders, and his blue eyes were striking against his tanned complexion. For some women, he might have been a 'good catch,' Kate supposed, but he wasn't her type.

'Sorry about this morning, Stephan, I—'

'You don't need to explain,' he interrupted gently. 'I'm not interested in excuses.'

'Look, maybe I could help in another way,' she offered hesitantly. 'I work in sales and marketing. What if I came up with a proper marketing plan for the club to bring in more people? These flyers aren't really doing much.'

He raised an eyebrow, sceptical but intrigued. 'Like what?'

Kate spent the rest of the day putting together a comprehensive plan. It included arranging interviews with local radio stations—Spanish, English and Scandinavian—alongside designing a competition to engage the audience. She suggested collaborating with package tour operators who could promote the club during their welcome meetings with new arrivals. In return, the reps and agents would receive free entry to the club for themselves and a few guests. She also proposed placing posters in hostels, tourist information centres and currency exchange booths—anywhere tourists might look.

To her relief, Stephan agreed to implement the ideas. He even did an excellent job during the radio interviews, promoting the club with enthusiasm. Kate managed to secure editorial slots in several local newspapers targeting expatriates and foreign residents.

Within weeks, the club was thriving. Word spread quickly, and soon, a lively, energetic crowd—locals and tourists alike—flocked to enjoy the music and vibrant atmosphere. Kate felt a sense of accomplishment. The project restored some of her confidence and reminded her of what she was capable of achieving.

But as the buzz of success faded, the questions about her future loomed larger. Stuart's email replayed in her mind. Did he truly not want her in his life? Was the 'experience living alone' just a convenient excuse to let her go?

One day, as she scanned the local paper, a small advert caught her eye:

Clairvoyant, palm and tarot card reader. Learn your destiny. Call now—what do you have to lose?

Instinctively, Kate picked up the phone. A soft Irish voice answered, calm and soothing. After a brief exchange about the fee and location, Kate hung up, feeling a flutter of nerves. She had never done anything like this before—not since her early twenties, when a group of friends had scared themselves silly with a makeshift Ouija board.

Kate asked her stepmum to come along for the drive, which turned out to be nearly two hours inland. The winding mountain road led them to a tiny hamlet. Her stepmum agreed to wait in the car while Kate went inside.

The house was warm and inviting, with a glowing fire in the hearth and the gentle scent of lavender filling the air. Kate felt an immediate sense of calm.

'Welcome. Come in and take a seat. There's water on the side if you'd like,' the woman said softly, her mellow tone immediately putting Kate at ease. It was as though her voice reached inside and soothed Kate's anxious thoughts, validating her decision to be here. She wasn't losing her mind or desperately clutching at straws for answers. No, this was more about seeking affirmation for the plans and ideas forming in her head.

The woman had striking black hair that fell gracefully to her waist, framing her face with an almost ethereal softness. Her strong jawline gave her an air of authority, while her piercing jet-blue eyes seemed to see right through Kate. She looked to be in her early to mid-forties, tall and slim, her presence both serene and commanding.

'May I see your hands?' the woman asked gently. She reached across the round table, its surface covered in a vibrant red felt that gave the room a warm, inviting glow. Taking Kate's hands, she turned them palm-up, her fingers gliding from Kate's wrists to her fingertips with a light, deliberate touch. There was an intimacy in the gesture that felt oddly comforting.

The woman retrieved a deck of tarot cards and, with practised ease, began to shuffle them. Before proceeding, she asked, 'Would you mind if I recorded our session? You're welcome to take the tape with you afterwards if you'd like.' Kate welcomed the idea; she didn't want to forget any of the insights that might emerge.

'You are on a journey of discovery,' the woman began, her voice calm yet resonant. 'This place is not your home; it is merely a transit point. Recently, something has happened that has caused you significant pain and self-doubt.' She turned each card with deliberate care, pausing momentarily before continuing. 'There has been a loss in your family, someone you loved deeply, someone who played an important role in your life. They feel your pain, and they want you to know they understand.'

Kate's eyes were fixed on the woman, her heart pounding as the words sank in. How could she possibly know this? Every detail was painfully true. Kate hadn't shared any personal information, not even in the brief phone call to confirm the appointment. It was uncanny.

The reading continued, each revelation more startling than the last. 'Your destiny lies in Asia,' the woman said, 'You may not yet know where or what you'll be doing, but your inner spirit is pulling you towards a new path in that part of the world.'

By the end of the session, Kate felt utterly drained, as though the emotional intensity of the reading had left her hollow. Seeing her exhaustion, the woman offered a bed to lie down and rest for a while.

'I would, but my stepmother is waiting for me in the car,' Kate replied with a grateful smile.

As she prepared to leave, Kate hesitated, then asked, 'How did you know all of this about me? Everything you've said is so accurate.'

The woman smiled knowingly. 'It's all in your hands and the cards,' she said quietly but with a conviction that left no room for doubt.

Kate shook her hand, thanked her and took the tape before heading back to the car. On the journey home, she and her stepmother listened to the recording, both stunned into silence by the accuracy of the reading. It was as though the woman had reached into Kate's life and laid it bare.

Chapter 24: The Last Goodbye

As weeks turned into months, Kate was surprised by how much she missed teaching English. Before leaving, she had ensured her students wouldn't be left without support, delegating her classes to two colleagues and providing detailed lesson plans. She had told the commander that family matters required her return home, and to her surprise, he had been understanding. Despite their non-native fluency, her colleagues were more than capable of continuing the lessons. Still, the thought of her classroom brought a pang of longing.

Kate's thoughts inevitably drifted to Stuart. That night, she wrote him a long letter. It wasn't angry or vindictive; it was thoughtful and reflective. She expressed hope for his future while acknowledging the truth: they could never truly turn back time. His actions had shattered her trust, and she doubted she could forgive, let alone forget, how he had sidelined her. She poured her feelings into the letter, knowing it was as much for herself as it was for him—a way to find closure.

Months passed. What had initially been six months of 'getting it out of his system' extended to eight. During that time, Kate focused on keeping herself afloat. She socialised sparingly, spending most of her time in quiet solitude, reflecting on what her next steps should be. Enough was enough. She couldn't keep putting her life on hold for someone who clearly didn't want to share their life with her.

She updated her CV and began applying for roles across Asia in her industry. She sent Stuart an email, asking if they could discuss their shared assets—the house and flat in the UK and all the entanglements of married life. There had to be closure; she couldn't continue living in limbo.

One morning, while scrolling through her emails, she came across one of Stuart's rare messages. She opened it, her breath catching as she read his words:

'Why am I doing this to you? I wanted time for myself, to act without considering anyone else, and it's been incredibly selfish and unfair. I don't want to lose the security of having you, but I also crave independence. I understand your frustration and anger because you've been unable to live a normal life for over six months now. You've been stronger than I ever imagined, but I know you've reached your limit. I'm at a crossroads, unsure of what I want or how to move forward. You're part of that confusion, and I know I've hurt you deeply. For that, I am sorry.'

Reading his words only solidified Kate's resolve. She had waited long enough, given him too much leeway, and endured too much pain. It was time to move forward, no matter how much it hurt.

Kate secured six interviews in London, arranging them all in the same week to minimise travel expenses. The lead-up to the trip was nerve-wracking; she experienced several severe panic attacks as the weight of everything bore down on her. Over the past eight months, she had become accustomed to the panic attacks, which occurred mostly during the night – the pain was excruciating, and even elevating herself onto her hands and knees and trying to breathe normally did not remove the pain. To make matters worse, Stuart emailed her to say he would be in the UK that same week and wanted to meet. It felt like a cruel twist of fate.

When she mentioned her job applications in Asia, Stuart's response was predictably selfish. He was furious, accusing her of jeopardising his own opportunities to relocate and remain working in Asia in the future.

'You can work in any industry, Kate. Why do you insist on staying in this one? I thought you'd be returning to the UK to live and work. Why are you still planning to stay in Asia?'

His words reignited her hurt and anger. How dare he assume she would uproot her life yet again to accommodate him? She had worked tirelessly to build her career, and she wasn't about to let him dictate her path. For once, she was putting herself first.

Kate knew her decision would bring challenges, but for the first time in a long while, she felt a glimmer of hope. Closure wasn't just about letting go of Stuart; it was about reclaiming her own life and charting a course towards a future that was truly hers.

Kate was overwhelmed. She knew she had to pull herself together; otherwise, she risked losing everything before she'd even been given a chance.

It was actually her former director who had informed her that Stuart was in the UK. He'd emailed to wish her well for her meeting with him later that week, hoping things would go smoothly between them.

However, Stuart had been in the UK for four days by the time Kate heard anything from him. Not once had he called or returned her messages. Yet, she heard from friends and family that he had managed to call them and even driven to Wales to visit mutual friends. It was also brought to Kate's attention that Stuart had attended the wedding of the woman he had first had an affair with, the very same woman he had been involved with while he'd wanted a taste of being single.

Eventually, Kate did hear from him—though by then, she knew she was being foolish. Against her better judgment, she let her heart take control and agreed to meet him after one of her interviews. She should have cancelled, should have backed out the moment she realised how little he had bothered to arrange anything or even inform her he was in town. It became painfully clear: if he couldn't be bothered to make an effort, there was no way he truly cared for her, let alone respected her.

The meeting itself was devastating. All it did was pull Kate back into an emotional abyss. The tears began to fall as soon as she saw him, and they didn't stop for the entire hour they spent together. It felt as if he had been deliberately pushing her further down, giving her another crushing blow: 'I need to be at the airport by 7 pm. Can you take me?'

It was like being punched in the stomach over and over again. Yet, pathetically, she agreed. He tried to hug her, but it was empty, strained—nothing like the warmth she'd once known. Kate watched as he walked towards the terminal, never once turning back. She felt a cold emptiness wash over her as the tears flowed freely, her heart shattering once more. She turned and drove away, the pain so sharp it seemed impossible to bear.

How Kate managed the rest of the week, let alone the interviews, was beyond her. Presentations, hours of tough questions—it was all a blur. Her exhaustion was evident. Puffy, red, swollen eyes, dark circles beneath them. Her face, haggard and drained, reflected the emotional turmoil she had been through.

Kate had stayed with her mother that week, and her support was nothing short of a blessing. She had been so understanding, and Kate couldn't help but be touched by how much their relationship had evolved. They were both strong women and this had sometimes caused their personalities to clash. Their time together in Vietnam and Bangkok had strengthened their bond, and they had become not just mother and daughter but friends. They had learnt not to be scared to show their love and affection for each other. Kate had also managed to catch up with her Chloe and her closest friends while in the UK. Liz, her sister-in-law, had been particularly amazing. She had been on Kate's side throughout the whole painful ordeal, offering a listening ear and unwavering support. Kate had confessed to Liz that she would have understood if Liz had decided to keep her distance, but Liz had been nothing but kind and loyal.

A few days after returning to Spain, Kate received five job offers out of the six she had applied for. Each one was in a different country, and two of them were for General Manager roles. After careful consideration, however, Kate had already decided on the plane: she didn't want the pressure and the overwhelming expectations that came with such a position, not at this stage in her life. The remaining three offers were for Sales and Marketing roles, all within the Asia Pacific region.

Exhausted but relieved, Kate flung her suitcase onto the bed and opened the window to let in the fresh sea air. She needed to breathe, to clear her head. As she settled down, ready to go through the job offers in more detail, her eye caught one email that stood out—an email from Stuart.

Dear Kate,

Whilst going through my paperwork, I have come across things such as your letters and photos which have been 'filed' and are waiting for me to respond. I still can't fully appreciate what I have put you through over all this time. With all the changes you have had to suffer but I know that I have been totally unfair to you, and you were/are the last person who deserved any of this. I am so sorry for all that I have put you through, and it is something that will stay with me forever. Fiona and I are getting on very well, but there is just something missing, or maybe there is doubt in my mind about what I really want. I did not lead a single life for very long, did I. I was not escaping you; be sure of that.

I hate being so selfish, and that is what caused what happened to you and me. I wanted and you suffered. I still have your photo in my office and still think of you often. It is strange how the smallest thing can make me go back to things we have done together over the many years we have been together.

You are going through your new start and all that entails, and I will be doing something similar.

I don't know where you got your strength from, but I admire you for it. You really are so strong (but not always). In one of your emails (that I did not reply to), you said:

'Stuart, this whole affair may not have affected or changed you personally, but it has had a big impact on me, and to be honest, it is still eating me up inside emotionally.'

I moved on emotionally to protect myself, and I am keeping a distance from those around me. Fiona is my way of protecting myself from myself. This is again unfair to Fiona. A part of me is feeling guilty about moving in with her when you are still trying to find a 'home' and somewhere that you feel at ease.

I can't turn back the clock and make it all better, and I am sure too much has happened to both of us; we can only look forward. I still think of us often and feel sad that I let this all happen to us. Sorry will never be enough to make it better, but I am truly sorry for what I have made you go through. Be strong, enjoy the lifestyle you wish to make in front of you, be selfish and look after number 1. You deserve it.

Stuart

Starring at the screen, Kate could feel the tears rolling down her cheeks. She began typing:

Stuart,

Why, why, why have you done that now after all these months of not talking or communicating with me. I knew that you had moved in with Fiona – news doesn't just stay in Hanoi as you well know. It was a shame that I heard it second-hand rather than from yourself. So much for wanting to experience life as a single person, setting up a new home in a new country and establishing a new circle of friends for yourself. That has never even happened. You just went on living in our home and then to our apartment in town, staying in the same job, same company and same country. You didn't even stay single as you were seeing the other woman before I left, giving you the space you demanded, continued seeing her and then when she left Hanoi, you found Fiona to share your life with whilst we are still married.

Sorry (not that I should even feel sorry for saying what actually happened). I am not going over old ground; I just needed to get this out.

Over the years we have been together, we have done some amazing things and had wonderful experiences. I was prepared to give 'us' another chance if you had not asked for an extension to be single for those extra four months. It was nearly eight months of me waiting whilst you enjoyed the single experience and trying to decide what you wanted. I think that was above and beyond patience and understanding.

Stuart, try and look at the positives and take something that you can hold onto and use in the next chapter of life from the years we shared. The hardest part for me during all this was not knowing what I had done wrong and being ignored and wondering what the other women in your life had that I could not give.

Learning to be single again is going to be so hard for me. If I ever meet someone in the future, I will certainly not be able to trust them for a long time. It's not going to be at the top of my agenda to seek a companion or get involved in another relationship. If it comes along unexpectedly, then I shall deal with it along the way.

Maybe we can use the time ahead of us to self-heal. It has been a tough time for you emotionally as well, and now is a time for reflection and inner peace. I could not have supported you and stood by you any more than I have.

Please let me know if I could have done something different. You said in the past and recently that I have been the motivating force behind many of the things that we have done and achieved together, but you forget that it's being together that motivated me to think the way I do sometimes and do different things with our lives. If we hadn't been together, yes, I would still have gone overseas to work and live, but it was much happier and more fun sharing the experience with you than as a single person.

Even after all that has happened, I will miss you, and my love for you won't disappear because our marriage has ended.

As they say:

When going through life and travelling in the direction

Of your dreams, the best way to get ahead is the simplest way

Take one step at a time

Don't look over your shoulder; if you do, you'll feel all the weight of all your yesterdays upon you. Don't worry about what lies ahead.

By the time you get there, the bend in the road or the crest of the hill, you're going to be better and stronger than you ever were before.

I am not sure which offer I am going to take. It will definitely be sales and marketing as it will make me get out and about and socialise, and it is a role in which I feel most comfortable. I have many contacts I can draw on – they will, I am confident will, follow me to my next company.

I am off for my daily walk along the beach, and hopefully, I will have made up my mind by the time I return to the apartment. I will send a list of the things that I would like to be packed up and shipped to wherever my next place called 'home will be.'

We can discuss (I hope) the splitting of our photos and personal and precious things that we have in a friendly way, no hatred or arguments.

My gut is telling me to go to a particular company. They were welcoming, open and honest about what they wanted for the future growth of their organisation. It looks exciting to be part of. The base country they are looking to recruit in feels like the right choice for me to start my next chapter and somehow learn and accept to be a single person again. I will go to the UK after New Year's Day and see mum, your sister and your dad. Catch up with a few close friends before I leave and start a new chapter of my life.

I am going to sign off now, make my decision today and get it finalised so that I can start the first week in January in one of these countries and let you know where my shipment needs to be sent.

Hongkong, India or Singapore.

Hopefully, now I will relax a little and try to enjoy Christmas and New Year celebrations with the clarity of knowing I have a path to follow, the security of a job and a new home to find.

Take care of yourself, always in my heart.

Kate xxx

PHOTO GALLERY

Vietnam in the 90s

1. Nghi Tam, Hanoi

2. Street Vendor Resting in Nghi Tam

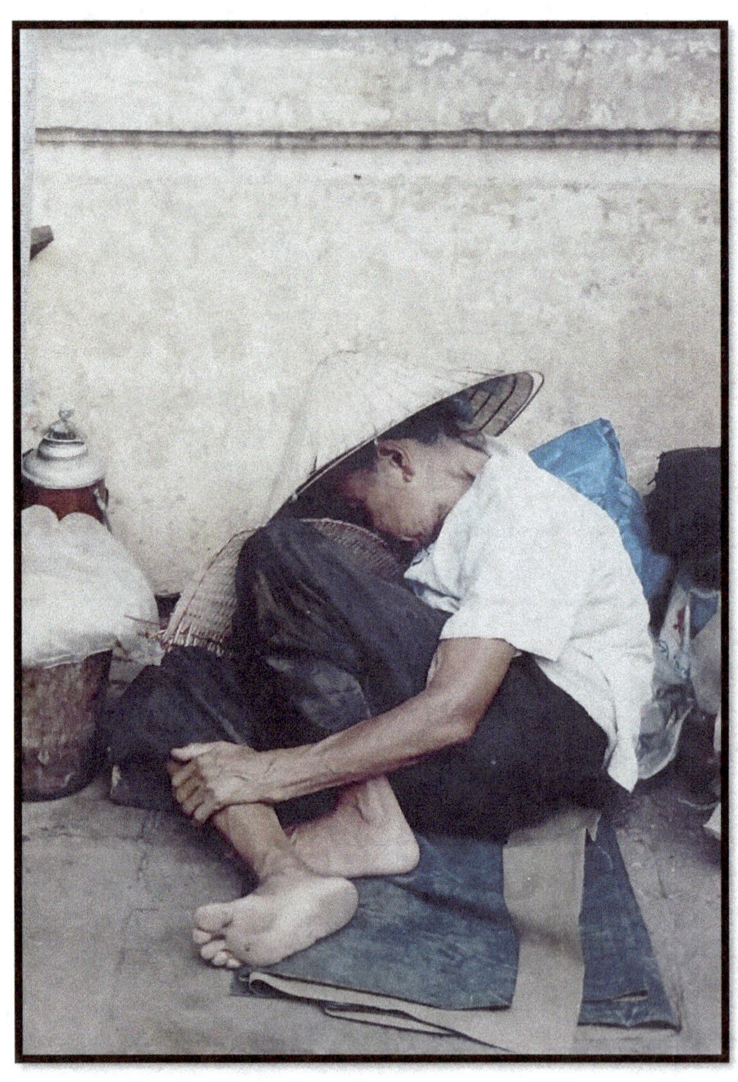

3. Chinese New Year in Hanoi, 1995

237

4. Fish Market in Hoi An

5. Wandering in Vietnam

6. Fishing Boats on Island Ha Long Bay

7. Heavenly Trip to Perfume Pagoda

8. One of Many Amazing Hash Routes

9. Two Guys Playing a Game

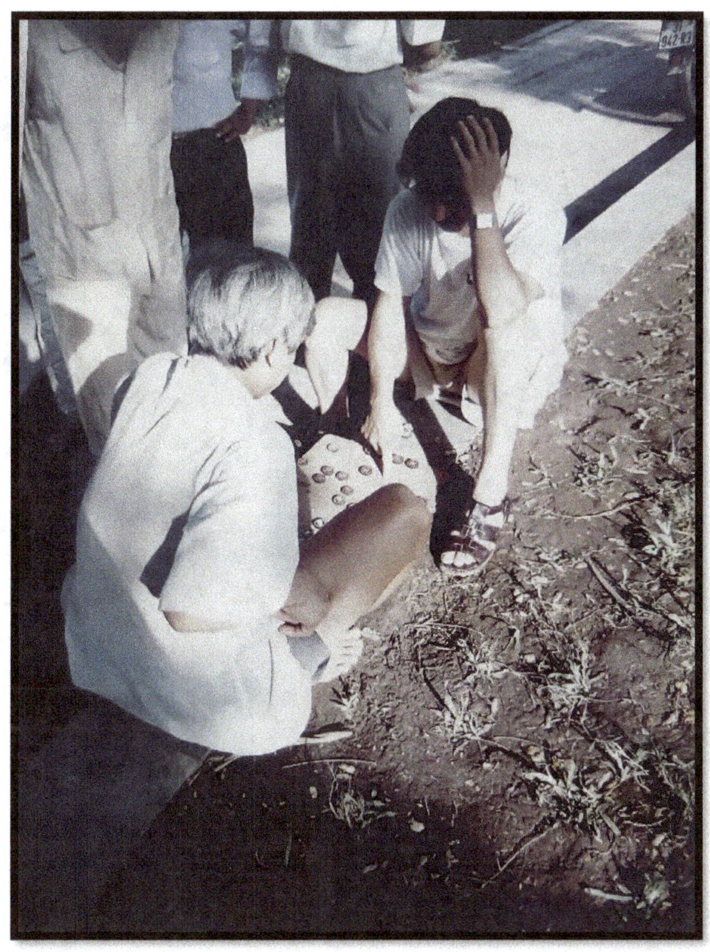

10.   The Hotel in Nha Trang – the trial run before opening

About the Author

With over twelve years of living and working in many countries, including Vietnam, Jane transports you fully into 'Kate's world,' the culture and experiences, including the dynamic International Corporate Business World.

Men and women of all ages and backgrounds will find this book a 'laugh out loud,' uplifting, thought-provoking, rollercoaster read. Her eloquent, heartfelt and almost poetic writing completely draws you in and keeps you turning the page, wanting to see what happens, from one challenge to the next, achievements and failures whilst following her dream.

Her writing opens your mind and heart to think, 'What if I followed my dream?' 'Could my dream come true?'

Born in Oxford, UK, now living in Hereford, UK. We are excited to be completely supporting and publishing Jane's first novel – as she said, it's for her grandchildren to read and be inspired to travel and live their dreams, as her Nan once told her.

Write Down Your Dreams

Write Down Your Dreams

Write Down Your Dreams